DANNY RHODES

Asboville

D1459189

DANNY RHODES

Asboville

Published in 2006 by
The Maia Press Limited
82 Forest Road
London E8 3BH
www.maiapress.com

Page 7: 'Mermaid Blues' lyrics by Tom McRae
published by Sony/ATV Music Publishing

ISBN 10: 1 904559 22 0
ISBN 13: 978 1 904559 22 1

A CIP catalogue record for this book is available from
the British Library

Printed and bound in Great Britain by Thanet Press

The Maia Press is indebted to Arts Council England
for financial support

To my family, friends and students

Over the water
There's you shining bright
In a sea of fools

Tom McRae, 'Mermaid Blues'

1

JB's court case was just two days away. He'd not thought about it much since the evening by the canal but now it was too close and not thinking about it was impossible. Everybody was saying it would be okay and that nothing would happen, like the time before and the time before that but it wasn't happening to them, it was happening to him and that made all the difference.

Evening saw the Jubilee Estate bathed in pink light. A lager can came tumbling up the alley. JB followed Scooby after it. Carla was lagging behind, busy on her mobile. JB had one ear on what Carla was saying and one ear on Scooby. The lager can came to a halt at the end of the alley and sat there on the open scrub that was the kiddie's playground, waiting to be kicked into oblivion.

'He's nothing mate,' said Scooby. He had his hoodie up and his hands buried in his pockets. 'He greened out after one puff. You should've seen him, throwing his guts up in Dicko's wheelie bin.'

'She's been talking to him all night.'

'She's like that with every lad. We all know who she's really into . . .'

'Who?'

Scooby stopped and looked JB in the eyes. The knowing stare was fixed and didn't falter for five seconds. JB stared back, desperately trying to hide it all.

'Yeah, right,' said Scooby. 'I wonder who it could be.'

JB turned away and his eyes fell on the lager can. Suddenly it was the centre of his world. He took a wild kick at it, sending it hurtling into the stratosphere. The two of them watched it sail over the railings. It came down on the bonnet of a car, causing the alarm to kick in and split the evening wide open.

They sprang back into the alley, Scooby first, JB behind. Carla was emerging from the shadows and Scooby bundled into her. The mobile phone went reeling and broke apart on the concrete. Carla screamed and scrambled after the different pieces while the two lads disappeared into the maze that was the estate.

A moment passed and then the sound of breathless laughter came rattling down the alley. The alarm was still wailing. A bloke in a tracksuit appeared from one of flats, face flushed, short of breath. He went to the car and the alarm fell silent. He stood there for a minute, looking in the direction of the alley. Then he spotted the dent on his bonnet. He ran his finger over the split paintwork.

'Little bastards,' he shouted at nobody.

The evening sky turned blood-red and the kiddies' playground was swamped with the colour. One of the swings trembled on its chains and the roundabout moved a little all on its own. A dog pushed through a gap in the railings and sniffed around on the scrub. A cat watched the dog from under a car, its tail twitching, ready to bolt. The dog found a crisp wrapper and buried its nose in it, then moved away towards where the bins were kept. A kid appeared on one of the balconies in just a nappy. It stood looking out from behind the black railings until its mother came out and dragged it back in. The child's screams bounced off the buildings and the dog barked back at the sound.

Smoke drifted up the alley from the fags the three of them were smoking, Carla still fumbling with her mobile, swearing under her breath. JB took the pieces from her and fitted them back together expertly while Scooby watched with a grin on his face. Suddenly he shouted.

'Dicko! Dicko! Over here!'

A tall, wiry boy stopped on the scrub in the exact spot where the dog had stopped to sniff the crisp packet. When he heard the call he turned towards the alley and started towards it, his long legs eating up the ground.

'Scoob my man . . .'

The tall boy and Scooby went through the nightly routine of the handshake, then it was JB's turn. Carla just nodded and went back to her mobile.

'What's up?' said Scoob.

'Nothing much. Just been with my old man. He's off night fishing at the canal. Got a tent and everything now.'

'Got any new DVDs?'

'Yeah, that Japanese horror thing . . .'

'Are you up for it?'

'Yeah, but no music. He'll kill me if the woman next door makes another complaint. The police were around again the other day.'

'I'll get some gear from mine.'

JB turned to Carla. They shared a glance as they both considered another night in Dicko's flat watching pirate DVDs and listening to Scooby after he'd smoked one of his monsters. The alternative was to hang around out here for another three hours.

'Got any tinnies?' asked Scooby.

Dicko shook his head.

'He took the last few with him or he's hidden them some place. There's not even any Jack Daniels. I checked after he went. Besides . . . if he comes home and there's nothing to drink . . .'

'I'll see what's in at ours. Jay?'

JB took a final drag on his cigarette, flicked it to the ground.

'No chance tonight. I'm skint.'

'Me too,' said Carla. 'I can't even afford any credit.'

'Looks like you two'll be on tea then,' said Scooby and he laughed, holding his finger and thumb together, bringing them to his lips like some old dear in a nursing home.

'I'll just watch the film,' said JB. 'I'm not up for a biggie anyhow.'

'Suit yourself,' said Scooby. 'But me and Dick are going for it tonight. Ain't that right?'

Dicko nodded, but JB could see behind it and he knew Carla could see behind it. Only Scooby couldn't see. He slapped Dicko on the back and the two of them set off down the alley. JB and Carla followed. JB stuck an arm over Carla's shoulder and pulled her towards him. She leant into the space between them automatically, filling it with her warmth, then the mobile sang out again and the moment disappeared.

'You can turn that off when we get there,' said Scooby. 'I want to watch this film . . .'

But Carla wasn't listening. She was falling back already, engrossed in another conversation with another faceless voice.

Scooby and Dicko were on the scrub now and Carla was still in the alley. JB came out of the shadows and stepped on to the grass, caught somewhere in between. Someone was playing drum and bass. The heavy sound bombarded the kiddies' playground and blasted through the railings, sending all other sounds reeling. The only sound that held its own against it was the high-pitched scream of the kid that had been on the balcony.

They cut through the garage block. Twenty garages, half of them empty shells, rusted metal doors twisted, mechanisms snapped and bent. Dark recesses stinking of piss. Rubbish piled in the corners, random stacks of junk in others, nothing useful, every ounce of use and misuse long since thought of and tried out to death. At the far end of the block a burned-out car, nothing but a blackened and charred frame, and eight garages down a second car, the windows already caved in, the wheels missing, bonnet up, crucial components removed, the roof covered in trainer prints of all shapes and sizes, kiddies' trainers too. JB picked up a brick and tossed it from hand to hand, waiting for Carla to catch up with him, thinking about the night at the canal, thinking about the court case and the worse that could happen. He thought about not throwing the brick for a second and then threw it anyway. It hit the driver's door and put a dent in the bodywork, one more dent to mix with the rest of the dents, caused by bricks and the heels of trainers where he and the others, all the others, even the little ones, had practised their karate kicks when the car had first parked there for the night, unaware of the fate that awaited it.

2

The fat guard had damp patches under his armpits. He was stood in the doorway to the compartment, filling it. The compartment already stank of sweat and now the guard had come in. The window was stuck fast where the rubber seal had perished and the air seemed to be getting heavier, as if the fat guard was pressing it against the window with his massive belly.

'You can't sit in here. First class only.'

'Yeah, well, there's no seats left anywhere else,' said JB.

'You can stand in the aisle,' said the guard. 'This is first class and it'll be full in a minute.'

'Twenty-seven quid this cost me and I've got all this stuff.'

JB pointed to the rack above his head. Two bags were shoved up there.

'Look, mate, in seven or eight stops there'll be plenty of room,' said the guard. 'Then you can stretch out. But for now it's first-class passengers in first-class seats.'

JB stood in the aisle, staring through the window. It was almost dark out. He was looking at the backs of hundreds of homes, at garden fences and broken sheds, washing lines and windows. As the train crawled out of the city he selected squares of light at random, focusing on them to see what was revealed. Each light was a window into some-body's world; a kitchen, a living room, a bedroom, a set of stairs. In some of the windows he saw people: a woman bent over an ironing board, an old couple sat watching TV, a kid jumping up and down on a sofa, swinging his arms like a maniac. Each view was fleeting, too quick to tell a real story, but JB saw stories anyway. It was like joining the dots in a book, building something from nothing. He was used to that. You built something from nothing and then somebody took it away from you. Like the fat guard, waiting for him to get his bags up on the shelf then coming in with his pathetic rules.

'Come on, mate. Give us a break.'

'Sorry, no can do. It's more than my job's worth.'

JB watched the windows and built his pictures until the buildings gave way to fields. Dusk settled like murky water until there was nothing to see at all. He stared at his own reflection instead. It was different from looking in a mirror. The cavities around his eyes were dark, two pools of shadow staring back from the glass, knowing stuff and threatening to reveal it. The feeling came again. It was like stomach cramp but worse because it only started in his stomach before spreading everywhere. It had come that morning when his mum had brought the bags into his room and it had grown as the day dragged on. It was funny. When they'd talked about it all, when they'd made their threats, when his mother had told him, then warned him, then pleaded with him, he'd simply brushed the feeling aside. Now that it was real the feeling had a grip on him and was tying his stomach in knots.

The image of the kid jumping up and down came back, causing him to think about Ellie, his half-sister. She was two years old. She came into his room and dragged the duvet away when he was trying to have a lie-in and screamed all morning when he had a hangover. His mum wouldn't say who the father was. They'd argued about it time and time again.

'He's not interested so it doesn't matter who the father is.'

'Dad's gonna want to know.'

'Jay, believe me, your dad only cares about one thing and that's himself.'

Two girls came up the carriage, clubbers, pulling their short skirts down in an effort to hide their legs, reeking of alcohol and perfume. The first girl shoved her head into the compartment with the dodgy window.

'Not that one, it stinks.'

They both squealed with laughter.

'Got any fags?' asked the second girl.

JB shook his head.

'Yeah, right.'

She sneered at him and then stumbled into the next carriage.

It was Thursday night. They'd be on the estate now, Scooby, Les, Craig, Missie. Carla would be there too, playing with her mobile. They'd be heading for the offy to get some bottles and Rizlas. Then they'd be on their way to Dicko's. He'd probably have some gear waiting, maybe a DVD. Or they'd be down at the kiddies' playground on the roundabout. Scooby would be spinning it and the girls would be yelling at him to pack it in, but they'd be laughing. All of them would be laughing.

JB punched the window. A blast of pain shot up his arm.

Were they talking about him? Scooby would be, Dicko too. Carla might be thinking about him but not saying much. She was like that. She kept things close to her. They'd be talking about him for sure. People weren't like text messages. They couldn't just be deleted, not even when they went away. Mates were mates. They stuck together and when one was away everybody else missed them like part of themselves were missing, until they came back and the gang was whole again. You couldn't just wipe a face from a place and expect everybody to forget that person existed. JB had lived on the estate all his life. He was part of it. It was part of him. They'd told him he was going to lose it and he'd laughed at them. They'd threatened and threatened, like they always did, like they'd threatened and threatened at school.

'So what? What are they gonna do?'

Now they'd done it.

Stuck the ASBO on him.

Made an example of him.

Made a criminal of him for standing in his own back yard.

The fat guard came back up the corridor. JB had to shove his whole body against the window to let him squeeze past.

'Still here, mate? There's loads of seats in second class. You're causing a bit of an obstruction.'

JB looked at the guard. His hand was throbbing and the urge to punch was almost overwhelming. He could do it and jump out of the train at the next stop, run off into the night, or he could leave the guard alone and let the train carry him to some place else. Or he could get off here with his bags and cross the platform, go back, find them. It'd be easy. And it'd be worth it too. For tonight it'd be worth it. It'd be worth it just to see their faces when he turned the corner.

Dad went out at three this morning. I heard the back door slam shut, as it always does when he's on a shout. He forgets, that's what he does, forgets other people are trying to sleep. It's no good telling him either because then he says I'm selfish and asks me where he went wrong bringing a child into the world who values her beauty sleep over the life of a drowning soul. But it hardly ever is a drowning soul. That's the point. If it is a bad one, he comes home and doesn't talk about it, so then we know and we live with it for a few days until we get to see it in the newspaper. After that everything goes back to normal. But it hardly ever is a bad one.

When he got home this evening he wasn't talking so I think last night might have been a bad one. I was sitting on my bed writing in this book when he came and stood at my door. I had my back to him but I knew he was there. I just carried on writing until I heard his foot-steps on the carpet and his bedroom door shut, then I went down-stairs to sit with Mum for a bit and watch TV. She wasn't saying much either so it looks like we're in for a few days of silence.

I've got an exam tomorrow. Sociology. I've not done anywhere near enough revision for it and I don't even care. I only do it for them. I only do it because they think it's the right path for me to be on, A levels, university, career. They won't talk about the gap year. Dad refuses. I think Mum would talk about it if he let her, but she's not strong enough. He probably thinks I've given up on it but I haven't. You can't give up on a dream that easily. Otherwise when would a dream ever come true?

3

JB was back in first class, stretched out with his feet on the seat opposite, drifting in and out of dreams. In one dream he was with them on the estate. They were all laughing. They were down at the kiddies' playground on the benches. Scooby was talking about taking a car for a ride. The woman who lived across the car park came out and told them to clear off. Scooby gave her the finger and they all laughed even more. The woman wrote something on a piece of paper and went back inside. It was a cold evening but the laughter and Scooby's antics were keeping them warm. JB had his hoodie up to keep the chill off his neck. Carla leaned towards him and put her head on his shoulder and he felt the familiar warm feeling run through him, then the dream stopped and he was on the train again and the warm feeling drained from his body like blood from a wound.

The compartment was cold now. The guard walked by and saw JB but didn't bother. He had a pie in his fist and some of the gravy was spilling down his fingers. JB watched him as he switched the pie to his other hand and licked the gravy into his mouth.

In his next dream his grandad was sat in the big chair in the living room. The TV was on loud, the washing machine humming. JB was sprawled on the sofa. His mother was in and out of the kitchen, drying dishes. Over the TV and the washing machine and the clattering of plates, his mother and his grandad were talking about him.

'It's important if they're teaching him something,' said his grandad. 'Otherwise it's a waste of time.'

'They don't teach us anything,' said JB.

'You see that's the sort of thing you put in his head,' said his mother.

'He could do something with his hands,' said his grandad. 'Instead of writing stuff and reading books that are hundreds of years old.'

'What?' JB asked.

'He can get a job in a factory.'

'They don't send kids off to factories these days. There aren't any factories. He needs qualifications.'

'What qualifications is he going to get? He needs to be using his hands, painting and decorating, that sort of thing.'

'Every kid in the school is going to be a painter and decorator, or a plumber or an electrician or a builder. Trouble is, none of them know a thing about any of that stuff. They think you just become one. He has to work.'

'I am working,' said JB.

'Don't give me that, Jay. You haven't a clue about work. I never see a book, only that thing.'

She pointed to the thin notebook sitting on the table with the chip wrappers.

'You don't take anything to school. I don't even know if you get there. Half the time you're home early . . .'

'I'm on restricted time,' said JB.

'Restricted time! They should bloody well lock you in until you do it . . .'

She slammed a pan down in the kitchen.

'Any more washing up? Or am I done?'

She started clearing the coffee table, one quick hand busy with the chip wrappers and sauce sachets, the other following behind with the dishcloth. JB jumped up and grabbed his notebook before it found its way to the dustbin.

'Quickest I've seen you move in a month,' she said.

JB could still see his grandad in that chair, the mug of tea on the dresser, the cigarette in the ashtray. He could hear the slow, laboured sound of his breathing, the way his chest struggled to expand with every breath. The memory of the day his grandad died lurched to attention inside of him. JB forced it back down, pummelled it into submission. Then it lay low again, waiting for the next opportunity.

Instead his grandad lifted himself up in his chair, his forearms straining, the veins bulging, fit to burst.

'It's all about knowing your station.'

'Eh?'

JB dragged his eyes from the TV.

Someone was adding up how much money they were going to make from buying a house and selling it again.

'Get to know your station, Jay,' whispered his grandad. 'Half the people around here think they're something they're not. They think the world owes them a living. They all want this and that and they spend their lives being miserable because they haven't got it. They're always whining and moaning. But the truth is they're lazy. They don't know the meaning of work. You need to get your hands dirty and earn a living. That's what people like us have to do. If you know your station you've got a foundation to build on . . .'

Get to know your station.

Get to know your station.

JB jumped up from the seat. The lights were off in the carriage. The train was pulling in. How long had he been sleeping?

The announcement crackled through the speaker.

'Broadgate is the next stop. This train terminates here.'

JB ran to the guard's van.

'What happened to Haycliffe?' he asked.

'You've missed it, mate. That was four stops back.'

'Why didn't you tell me?'

'I can't remember every person and where they're going. Bloody hell, if I could do you think I'd be doing this for a living?'

'Can I get a train back?' he asked.

The fat guard looked at his watch.

'Not tonight. You'll have to wait till tomorrow. Or get a taxi.'

'Right,' said JB. 'Like I can afford one.'

The fat guard nodded.

'Yeah. Bloody expensive these days.'

The station lobby was deserted. There was just the bleaching light and the tiled floor that reflected the light back up. JB walked over the tiles, his hollow footsteps filling the hard space. He reached the nearest bench and sat on it, trying to think what to do. After five minutes another guard came over. He was carrying a bunch of keys.

'Station's closing, mate.'

'I've missed my train,' said JB.

'Where's that to?'

'Haycliffe.'

'First one's at seven in the morning.'

JB sat looking at the man.

'Well, I can't let you stay in here. I've got to lock up.'

'I could just sit here.'

'Sorry, mate. Rules are the station's closed.'

The guard waited for JB to exit the place and then closed the door behind him. There was the clink and rattle of keys, the metallic clack of the lock dropping in and then the rattle of keys again. A minute later the lights in the lobby went off and the place was swallowed by darkness.

The station was high up on top of the town. JB could see the line of lights that marked the harbour. A taxi would cost him thirty quid at this time, maybe more. He only had fifty to last forever. There was no way he was spending over half on a taxi. He sat on his bags and pulled his hoodie tighter but the security he was seeking failed to settle over him. He'd been cold when he woke on the train, now the cold was tightening its grip. A breeze was coming in off the sea, biting at all the exposed skin it could find.

He noticed a phone box at the end of the building, the sort that stood on legs and let the air in. JB got himself inside and sat down on the concrete, pulling his knees up to his chest to try to keep warm. For a minute it was better, but sitting meant his jeans rode up at the ankles and the breeze found its way however he tried. His knees and neck ached too. He had to move position every minute and finding comfort was hopeless.

Soon after he got curled up a car raced into the car park. It was full of lads. They were pumping out heavy base and swigging at cans of beer. The car skidded as the driver threw it around the tarmac in a wild figure-of-eight. Cans flew out of the window, beer spraying in the headlights. Twice the headlights lit up the telephone box and twice JB had to huddle down, a stricken rabbit, his heart thumping. Long after the car had gone, he found himself listening to its squealing tyres, measuring the distance each time it cornered, trying to work out if it had gone for good or was making its way back.

Between tiny slivers of sleep, JB watched the time crawl on his mobile. Nobody called him, not even Carla. He hated himself for not having any credit. He really needed to talk to Carla, to tell her about the fat guard and the club girls, to let her know he was okay. Carla would make it different, make it feel like it was happening to someone else. She'd laugh and call up the others, tell them that JB had called, tell them how he was spending a night in a telephone box.

I spoke to Dad about not going to university. He hit the roof and then tried blaming Mum, accused her of putting ideas in my head. I told him I wanted to take a year out, that's all, maybe go and see the world. He wouldn't listen. I don't know why he got at Mum. Maybe because she did it before they were married. She didn't go around the world but she travelled around Europe. She went to Rome and Madrid and Berlin. She showed me her photos once. She was pretty then. She had a sparkle in her eye.

Dad doesn't understand. He's lived here all his life. I don't think he even wants me to go to London. I think that's too far for him. The local university would be better in his eyes but there's no way I'm staying close. I'm sick of the place, sick of the people, sick of being here.

It's carnival week soon. They've put the flags up already. They had the same flags when I was six years old. It's a cheap little place. They rave on about how hip it is with its galleries and restaurants, but they can't even buy some new flags.

I had a row with Dad about it. When I mentioned the flags he went crazy. He said I was spoilt. He said my head was growing too big and if I wasn't careful I'd lose touch with my roots, that he'd seen people who'd done that before. He said they're the ones who drive their fancy cars into town on a Friday and spend their money in the fancy restaurants none of the locals can afford and sit on the beach in the summer like they own the damn place. He said they should try a hard day's work instead of making money from other people's money and buying all the property so that none of the locals can afford to live in the damn town they grew up in. He went on and on about it and told me if I ever turned out like them he'd disown me. Mum went into the kitchen and he started shouting through at her, asking her how come his daughter had turned out this way and telling her there were some opinions flying about the house that had no right to be there.

He thinks I'm ten years old. He doesn't understand my opinions. He doesn't even try. He thinks girls should shut up and listen to their fathers. Mum says he's changed since they were married. She says he used to talk about getting out all of the time but the town sucked his soul out. She says the boat dragged the last adventure out of him. She says all the crew members are the same and if a man spends too much time around people who think in a certain way and behave in a certain way then he eventually ends up like them. And that's the thing that frightens me the most, spending too much time here and being trapped by it, waking up one day to find myself just like everybody else.

4

Dreams washed over him, came and went like the tide.

His mother in the kitchen.

'I'm sending you away. You heard what they said down there. Next time is the last time . . .'

Dicko on the swings, smoking, taking deep drags, blowing the smoke out of his lungs into the evening, his long legs folded under him. Scooby on the roundabout. Craig trying to spin it fast and Scooby standing on it. Scooby spreading his arms out and trying to do it with his eyes closed. Craig spinning it faster, sending Scooby flying.

'Oi!'

JB talking to Dicko while Scooby chased Craig and rugby-tackled him to the ground by the railings.

'What if they send me down?'

'Prison? Nah, not for throwing eggs and not for breaking a window either . . .'

'Yeah, but what about the car?'

'You weren't driving the car.'

'I can't prove it . . .'

'Neither can they.'

Another drag.

'How many warnings have you had?'

'A couple.'

'Well then.'

'Well then what?'

'They won't do anything yet. What about visits?'

'One I think, after that time with the garden.'

'You mean with that fencing? That was pathetic.'

'That was her up there.'

JB pointed to the flat across the car park. The woman was sat in the window, watching.

'Forget that. That was nothing. They know what she's like.'

Carla on their bench, snuggling up to him.

'Keep me warm, Jay. I'm freezing.'

Something always threatening to happen between them, nothing ever happening between them.

The policeman by the canal.

A knee pressed into his back, forcing him face down into the gravel that was the towpath. Some of the little stones in his mouth. The metallic taste of blood each time he opened his mouth to shout, cutting himself again and again on the stones. And all the while the policeman pressing and pressing his knee into JB's kidneys until the pain was unbearable.

JB sat up, blood rushing to his head. His knees and back were aching. His bags were at his feet and he'd been using his hoodie as a pillow. It was screwed up on the seat beside him.

They'd let him get on the train as soon as the station opened. It was the first of the day and it had been empty then. Now other people were on board and the train was on the move. A lot of the passengers were suited up for the city, reading newspapers or flicking through diaries and memo pads. The man opposite was chewing on a bacon roll. The smell of it entered JB's nostrils and he felt his stomach lurch, crying out for breakfast. He looked out of the window and tried not to think about it. The train rounded a long sweeping bend and there was the coastline, a grey scar of a beach, the ocean looking like a field of mud.

'Haycliffe will be the next stop.'

JB made his way to the door. Nobody else seemed to be moving and nobody got up as the train pulled in. The platform was full of people though, all waiting to get on. The suits were on all sides of him as he stepped down. He had to push past them, ignoring the looks they gave him for daring to try and get off where they were trying to get on. Doors slammed up and down the train and the train went on its way. Pretty soon the platform was deserted, apart from a family of pigeons up in the metal rafters. They watched JB as he struggled with his bags, their chests rising and falling like tiny inflatable balloons, then they hopped down to see what scraps had been left behind.

JB reached the station exit. Two kids weighed down with bulging schoolbags squeezed past him, their faces flushed red with the effort of it all. JB turned to watch them as they raced to the empty platforms, memories of his own schooldays flooding over him.

The hall was half the size of an aircraft hanger and it was full of girls and lads, each sat at a desk in a row with an evenly measured space between them, each pointing the same direction, each waiting silently for the signal to begin.

There was no heating and the morning was chilled. Those with short sleeves were rubbing their arms and blowing warm air into their palms, doing what they could to fight it.

JB came in with a minute to spare, his eyes red from the cold wind, sleet, lack of sleep. They'd been at Dicko's all night on the Playstation, the hours fizzing by. He had a headache from the vodka he'd downed and the smoke he'd breathed. Eyes darted in his direction as he skirted those already seated. The clowns of the last five years were suddenly vacant. They sat like everybody else, dormant and expressionless, as if the very life-blood they existed on had been sucked out of them.

There were three booklets on his desk and a little yellow tag with his name on. When he sat down the plastic seat was icy cold. When he touched the metal frame he felt his fingers threaten to stick to it. He shuffled for comfort. The clock ticked on a notch, the sound echoing out over the heads of the mass, resounding back off the far wall, the only indication that time was still passing.

JB turned his head to the left, where one desk remained empty. It was Scooby's. A teacher was stood over it, signalling to another teacher at the front, who shrugged impassively. The teacher by the desk picked up the booklets and the little yellow tag and carried them to the front. JB laughed to himself. Scooby wasn't coming. He was flat out on Dicko's sofa.

JB pulled himself deeper into his hoodie and waited, one hand busy with his one biro, which was chewed and cracked, pathetic in its existence, the blue plastic tube sticking out of the top, bent over at an angle, the ink level in the tube perilously low. Not that it mattered. The exam was maths. There was nothing in it he knew about.

The teacher who'd been at Scooby's desk came over, a thin grey-haired rake of a man. He stopped in front of the desk and leaned in close, his breath stinking of fags.

'Have you seen him?'

JB shook his head.

'Take the coat off,' whispered the teacher. 'And we can get this thing started.'

JB leaned back in his chair.

'It's cold,' he said.

'Doesn't matter,' said the teacher. 'Take it off.'

JB looked around to see others staring back, eyes boring into his eyes, sending messages with those eyes. He stood up and started to lift the hoodie over his head, felt the cold nip at his exposed skin, pulled the hoodie back on and slumped into the chair. The teacher watched the whole performance and glanced at the clock.

'Jason,' he said. 'If you don't take the jacket off you will have to leave.'

JB breathed out, a long deep breath that showed as a mist in the air in front of him.

'See?'

'Everyone's in the same boat,' said the teacher.

'You take your jacket off then.'

A murmur took life in the hall and started to spread, whispers and mumbles, suppressed laughter. More heads turned and this time when the clock clicked on a notch nobody noticed. Nobody except the teacher.

'I'm not arguing with you. Two hundred people are waiting and you are now causing a disruption. Take the coat off or leave.'

'I'll leave,' said JB.

He pushed back his chair, the legs tearing across the glazed flooring, the sound ripping through the murmurs, punctuating the moment. And then he marched to the door, more aware of the drama now, aware that there was no going back, trying to think of something to say but thinking of nothing until he reached the door, where he turned and shouted back across the room.

'I'll fail then!'

As soon as he got beyond the door the wind bit again. He pulled his hoodie up and started across the car park, heading for the bus stop, dodging the puddles, watching the cars rush by on the Parkway, the hiss of tyres on tarmac the dominant sound, a piercing noise that repeated itself endlessly like the rush of an angry tide.

5

'Lowes Field? No worries.'

The taxi driver had muscular forearms and stubby fingers, as though someone had cut the ends off each one with a blunt pair of scissors. He had a faded tattoo on the inside of his right arm. The thick black hairs covering it made it hard to work out. JB took little sideways glances at it when the driver was concentrating on the road, but the driver saw.

'I was in the army,' he said. 'Everybody had one. Bloody thing reminds me all the time. You want my advice, don't bother with 'em. You remember the good times anyway, you don't need tattoos.'

The taxi wormed its way through the town. There was a line of terraced houses on both sides and cars were parked in every space. A lot of the cars had new registration numbers. They didn't match the scrubby houses they were parked in front of. The tick-tick of the indicator marked their turning into another street that was exactly the same as the one before, a line of houses, cars parked in front. Another set of tick-ticks, another street, another set of houses, cars parked in front.

'You can't get parked anywhere any more and it's not even summer,' said the driver. His stubby fingers were tightly folded around the steering wheel. There was a look in his eyes that was meant for a war zone somewhere.

They reached a T-junction that met the High Street. At regular intervals between the buildings, strips of coloured flags were whipping back and forth in the breeze. The taxi shot across into another street and JB had just enough time to see the word 'Carnival' written in fiery red letters, but then came the terraced houses and cars again.

The road widened and the buildings started to space out. These were bigger houses, houses behind stone walls and iron gates, detached houses with gravel driveways and double garages. JB started getting ideas but before these ideas could form into anything the taxi shot out of the neighborhood and into open country.

£4.10 . . . £4.50 . . . £4.90 . . .

JB watched the red digits. He felt for the cash in his pocket and started doing the sums in his head.

They were on the beach road. On the right was a grass embankment topped with a concrete wall. Steps were cut into the grass bank at regular intervals along it. There were wooden posts and metal banister rails at each set of steps. On the left was a line of chalets. Beyond the chalets the land was flat, clumped grasses holding against the breeze, clouds rolling in low from the sea. The chalets gave way to a line of conifer trees, all cut to shape, thick with foliage, forming a wall as solid as the concrete wall opposite. Half a mile later there was a gap in the conifers, a gate, a white hut and a 'Welcome' sign.

'That's the holiday village,' said the taxi driver as they raced past. 'Still as popular as ever. You wouldn't believe it. Who wants to visit this place when you can get on a plane and go and live it up in Spain for a week? Sex on the beach . . .'

He started singing the song, tapping those stubby fingers on the steering wheel.

The numbers were on £6.10 when the taxi driver shifted down and the tick-tick of the indicator started up again.

'Lowes Field,' said the driver.

JB was staring at a cluster of old caravans, scattered randomly over an area the size of a football pitch, TV and radio aerials sticking up like weird antennae; a rusted free-standing washing line, some of the cables broken and useless, others littered with multi-coloured pegs, none of the pegs holding any washing; a crumbling outhouse with a corrugated tin roof, two great black holes in it, tarpaulin sheets draped over the holes, rusting nails sticking out; a single tree standing alone amongst all of this and, towering over the lot, a huge electricity pylon, an alien invader, the clouds creating the illusion that it was about to topple and crush everything beneath it.

'What number?' asked the driver.

'Dunno,' said JB. He forked a tenner out of his pocket and handed it over. The driver glanced at the charge and then gave JB a fiver back.

'You look like you need it,' he said.

6

The taxi wheeled around in the gravel, sending a dust cloud of sand up into the air. It blew across the caravan site and into JB's eyes.

He stood at the gate for ten minutes, not knowing what to do. One or two of the net curtains twitched inside the caravans but nobody came out. From not so far away came the gentle rush and hiss of the tide on the beach.

Suddenly there was a crashing sound behind him. JB span around, danger signals flashing like they did on the estate. A great mutt of a dog came bounding towards him, barking madly. More curtains twitched.

'Leave it!'

The dog stopped. It turned in a wide circle, kicking up more sand and dust.

An old man stepped down from one of the caravans. He was carrying a spade in one hand and a plastic bag in the other. He moved freely, not like the oldies on the estate, and as he approached JB saw the resemblance to his grandad.

'What the bloody hell happened to you?' asked the old man.

'Fell asleep on the train,' said JB.

JB ate beans on toast. His uncle told him to get some sleep, left him to it and went off somewhere with his spade. The caravan was tiny. There were two sets of seats and a table at one end. The kitchen was in the middle, just a two-ring hob, a tiny fridge and a sink. At the far end was the old man's bed. The sheets were worn and covered in dog hair. JB's bed doubled as the sofa. He grabbed the handle down by his ankles and turned it upwards. The table started to fold away. So this was what the future held. Fold away the table, pull out the cushions, close the curtain that divided the room and pretend you weren't sleeping in a caravan in the middle of nowhere next to an old man you didn't know and a dog you didn't want to know. Pretend your friends were in the next room drinking beer or your mum was frying up some chips. Pretend you had a life.

JB pulled the curtain across, made up his bed and collapsed on it. He could hear the dog barking somewhere outside, the surf on the beach. It didn't come to him until later that the hut out in the yard with the tarpaulin roof was the toilet. When it did he didn't care. He was already planning his escape.

7

Sunday morning. His uncle clunking around on the other side of the curtain, the dog sniffing and scratching, the smell of eggs on the burner. JB stuck his head out.

'You're a lucky boy. They could have put you away. The social worker's due next week. I've got the name here somewhere.'

His uncle reached under the bed and pulled out a pile of envelopes.

'Here. Swallow. Barry Swallow. That's your man.'

JB shrugged.

'He'll be checking all this out. Don't know what for. I told them plain enough it wasn't the Hilton. Anyway, get those down you and I'll show you the job.'

The job was to paint beach huts.

'There's eighty-seven,' said his uncle. 'I did the insides last spring so this year it's the outsides. It's best to aim for one a day. That's what I agreed with the owners' club.'

'I'm not doing it,' said JB, but his voice just drifted off on the breeze and his uncle either didn't hear or chose to ignore it.

'You can start later, after I've shown you where the stuff is kept. They told me if you don't do it I'm to report you. I said that's exactly what I'll do. It's not a bad job. Just take it nice and steady, that's all.'

An hour later JB carried the ladder from the storage shed to the first hut and set it against it, working the feet of the ladder down into the pebbles so it was firm and secure to climb. The paint tins were stacked at the back of the shed in the darkest part. They were covered in dust. Tired old cobwebs were strung between them. JB thought about the spiders that made them. It made his skin crawl.

A night back in the city when he was very young, his mother and father arguing in the next room. He'd turned over in his bed, not quite with it, found himself face to face with the biggest spider in the universe. It was sitting there on the wall, an inch from his nose. He'd screamed and screamed. His mum came rushing in. The spider scuttled down the side of the bed and his mum couldn't see it anywhere.

'It's just a bloody spider,' his father kept shouting, over and over again.

'Well, he's scared of them. You should be in here . . .'

'Tell him to stop thinking about it and go back to sleep. It's just a bloody spider . . .'

The shouting went on like that. It had always been like that, spiders or no spiders.

JB grabbed the nearest tin of paint and a brush from the shelf. He backed out into the morning light. He dusted the paint tin down and checked the colour on the label. Summer Red. It was as easy as that.

The first hut would be Summer Red. He pulled an old pen-knife from the cobwebs and forced the lid from the paint tin with it. Then he gave the paint a stir with a stick he found on the beach. At first the paint didn't look red, it was brown instead, but as he stirred it transformed itself and the real colour came to the surface. It was nine-thirty in the morning on the first day. The line of huts stretched down the beach, a long thin snake with a skin of flaking colours.

Hours passed. Each time he dipped the brush into the paint and lifted it to the wood it ran from the brush and ended up falling in thick blobs on to the sea wall. He made adjustments. Now there wasn't enough paint and after one sweep the brush was dry. He had to go over the same area twice, three times, four times. His wrist ached. His whole arm started to emit a dull throb that only went away when he rested. As soon as he felt ready and lifted his arm to start up again the pain came back. And the pain grew with the crawling hours, making the job impossible.

Late afternoon. His uncle came down to the huts. JB watched him looking at the paint on the sea wall, the paint on the sides of the tin, the paint on his clothes. Hut number one was half-done at best and some of the streaks were obvious.

The voice of his old boxing coach filled his head.

'Get in the first punch. Get one in before he's ready. Put a doubt in his mind.'

So JB did.

'What?' he asked.

His voice was aggressive and defensive, a signal to his uncle to back off, but his uncle simply leaned in and inspected the hut closer.

'It's only a beach hut!'

His uncle turned to face him.

'Never "only", Jay. Not when it's your living.'

'It's not my living . . .'

'It is for the next few months. Besides, it's my living. Anyway. You're doing okay. A little slow but okay.'

'Slow! My arm's killing me.'

'You'll get used to it. Trick is to use just the right amount of paint. Then it's easy.'

'Whatever,' said JB shaking his arm.

'Give it another hour,' said his uncle. 'And make sure you lock the shed before you come back. You remember where the key is?'

Boredom. Repetition. Paint. Beach huts.

Shed number one – Red.

Shed number two – Yellow.

Shed number three – Green.

After three days he was sick of the place.

8

Shed number four (red again). A gang of lads appeared. He spotted them a mile off, four of them on the sea wall. Caps and trainers, hand gestures. He heard their voices on the wind, the shouts and the swearing. They were his age and it made him nervous to be out here alone. When he was certain they were coming all the way he ducked into the paint shed, spiders or no spiders . . .

He pulled the door shut and hid behind it, quick eyes piercing the gap between the door and the frame. He stuffed the pen-knife in his pocket too, just so it was in there.

If Scooby was here . . . if Dicko was here . . .

But they weren't.

The gang of lads passed by the crack. One of them spotted the tin of paint on the trestle. The fattest took a run at it, kicked it into the air, sending the paint spraying on to the sea wall and the fifth hut. Then they ran, laughing and hooting.

JB waited until they were gone before emerging from his hiding place. The paint was mostly on the porch of hut number five. It looked like somebody's head had been kicked in. He took a brush and worked it into the paint, started spreading it while it was still wet. He did that until his uncle came down.

'What happened?'

JB ignored him.

'Well, you can't have two the same next to each other,' he said.

'Why not?'

'Rules,' said his uncle.

'Forget the rules.'

'Not if you want to make any money. That's the way it works. Follow the rules, get paid at the end.'

'Are you going to pay me then?'

'Sure. I'll pay you with a roof over your head and three meals a day.'

'What am I going to do with this one?'

'Blue. Blue will work. It's darker. Let that dry and paint over it. And be careful of the concrete. You don't want to be letting that dry. Get some turps on it while it's still wet and throw some buckets of water on it. Bloody hell, you'll have me shot.'

The lads came back in the afternoon. By the time JB saw them it was too late. The fat one, the one that had kicked the tin, stopped at the fifth hut, looked JB up and down.

'Why are you painting this hut red, mate?'

He turned to the others, cracking up. They started up too.

'You should get spray cans.'

All of them.

'We'll tag 'em.'

Jabbing at each other.

'Yeah right. Everybody wants to see your tag.'

'My tag is the best . . .'

'Your tag is weak.'

On they went, down the sea wall, disappearing into the landscape, specks in the distance.

JB watched them go, his head full of the estate.

Shouting.

A crowd down at the kiddies' playground. Adults mostly. JB, Scooby, Carla, Missie. Some others he couldn't remember. A woman screaming.

'They smashed my bloody window.'

'It wasn't us!'

'Always hanging around. Look at the place. It's meant to be for the kids!'

'They are kids!'

'They're not kids, they're animals.'

'My kids are too scared to come down here . . .'

'Night after night . . . .'

'The swings are broken . . .'

'Well, don't you go blaming my son. Your daughter's hardly Miss Innocent.'

'Graffiti everywhere!'

'You should hear the language. It's disgusting . . .'

'Don't you go slagging off my daughter, you stupid cow.'

'You have it on your doorstep . . .'

'You're calling me a cow. A slag like you . . .'

Flashing lights. Two police cars.

'Where are you when they're terrorising the place?'

'Just go inside, please . . .'

'Too bloody busy handing out speeding tickets . . .'

'She called my daughter a slag . . .'

'Please, just go inside . . .'

Missie slipping off with her mother. Scooby, Carla and JB with the police, giving names, Scooby giving a false one but JB not having the nerve.

Scooby having a crack at him.

'You tosser. Just make one up.'

'I couldn't think of one.'

The police taking him home. His mother laying punches on him in the bedroom. JB laughing at her. Ellie waking up and screaming. His mother in tears.

Early evening. JB scrambled through the sea grass, heading back to the caravan. The fourth hut was finished, the fifth a mess. He stopped on the slope and looked back at them, the sun dropping over the ocean, shadows stretching out towards him. Every part of him ached and he was covered in red paint.

Steam was rising from the tiny chimney on the roof of the caravan and when he opened the door the dog nearly bowled him over. His uncle was at the hob, cooking sausages. The smell filled the caravan and made JB's mouth water.

'Look what the cat dragged in,' said his uncle. 'Looks like you've been sweating blood.'

JB grunted and sat down.

'You need to get two plates, two knives and two forks. A glass each. Sausage and mash coming up. Onion gravy if we're lucky . . . from a packet, mind . . .'

The dog settled under the table at JB's feet. JB reached down and patted its head for a minute then got the plates and everything ready. After that he fished for his mobile. Still no calls. He got up, stepped out of the caravan into the yard. He needed some credit. He needed to call them, just to talk, just to hear their voices and laugh like the lads on the beach had laughed. He stared down at the flashing signal on his mobile, a tiny green heartbeat blinking in the fading light. It was like they'd forgotten him. He knew they hadn't but it was like that.

What it is, is row upon row of terraced houses. Everybody packed in like sardines in a tin, but dead like sardines, so that nobody speaks to each other. Everybody in their own silent place. Nobody talking about the big stuff, the news, politics, because it's too heavy, because they don't understand it, because they're fed up of thinking about it and it never tells them anything they don't already know.

The High Street forever busy, people spending money. Spending, spending, spending. Like a disease.

Pavements cracked. Wheelie bins in the gutter. Streets like rabbit runs. Lads in cars racing around the warren at crazy speeds. Wheels screeching at stupid times of the night. Kids roaming around, nowhere to go, nothing to do, spoiling for fags, beer, alcopops, dope. That's all the rage now. It doesn't matter if you're thirteen. Baseball caps, puffa jackets, hoodies, fake designer wear, hooped earrings on the girls, aggressive posture and performance. Gangs everywhere. Outside the off-licence, outside the chip shop. Sex talk. Swearing. Aggravation.

The adults are no better. Fights every Friday and Saturday, in the kebab house, at the taxi rank. Blood on Ben Sherman. Chants and taunts. Police sirens wailing. But it's not America. It's not even a city. Whatever it's trying to be it's easy to see through. How can Dad defend it? How can he tell me I'd be better off here? How can he call this living?

9

'So what happened?'

JB was on the fifth shed (blue now, hiding the red underneath). Dark colours were easier. It was easier to see where he'd been and where he was going. He was sat cross-legged, working on the steps. The sun was hot, the sea still, a million diamonds shimmering. He'd been up since dawn, trying to finish early. He'd made a plan and was putting it into play. Or he had been. Now Swallow had turned up and it looked like his plan was going to the dogs.

'What do you mean?' asked JB. He was trying his best to be interested, trying to say all the right things so it would be over.

Swallow had turned up that morning. He'd come around the beach huts and sat himself on the sea wall. For ten minutes he just sat there staring at the sea until JB called over to him.

'You looking for someone?'

'Who, me?' Swallow shuffled around on his backside, squinted in the sunlight. 'Just admiring the view. Pretty impressive.'

'Today, maybe . . .'

'Summer's coming. They say it's going to be a scorcher.'

Swallow got to his feet and raised a hand. JB backed up a step. Once again the signals flashed in his head.

'I take it you're Jay. I'm Barry Swallow. I'm assigned to you.'

That had been two hours ago and Swallow was still hanging around. All the time JB worked on the paint job and now he was thinking about the train. But Swallow just kept asking questions. How was he coping? How did he feel? Was he sleeping okay? Eating okay? Was there anything he wanted that Swallow could get for him? JB had laughed at that. There were a hundred things Swallow *could* get for him but none that Swallow *would* get for him.

Now he was asking questions about before.

'You don't have to tell me,' Swallow said. 'It just helps. I've read the case notes but I want to hear your story.'

'Nothing happened. There's nothing.'

'Jay, you can trust me. I'm not here to judge.'

'There was nothing. Just stuff. It's pathetic. I've got to finish this hut.'

Swallow sat himself on the sea wall again.

'If you go back and they catch you, you realise that's it, Jay. They'll stick you in a detention centre.'

'So what have I got to lose? They've got me stitched up whatever. Not to cross the boundary between King George Court and Queen Mary's Road. What's all that about?'

'Because they don't want you going home,' said Swallow.

'It's a joke. How can you stop someone going home? What about my rights?'

'What about them? It doesn't look like you have any.'

'A sick joke . . .'

'Are you laughing? I'm not. I don't think it's fair either but then who cares what I think? What I know is that you have to keep your nose clean and not try to make out you're laughing at them. Because if you do that and they catch you . . .'

JB stopped painting.

'They'd have to catch me . . .'

'They caught you before.'

A moment of silence dropped into place between them, held its own, was broken by Swallow's soft voice.

'Listen, I'm off but I'll be back next week. Your uncle's doing his bit. Think about talking to me. I'm good at my job. I can help.'

He slipped down the side of the blue hut and disappeared. JB shrugged and went back to painting for ten seconds then got up and raced after him. He caught him in the sea grass.

'How did you know?'

'Know what? That you're planning to go back? Like I said, Jay, I'm good at my job,' Swallow grinned. 'Plus, your uncle told me you missed breakfast this morning and that normally you won't budge from your pit until you smell it on the burner. There had to be a reason.'

By 3.30 p.m. the hut was finished and JB was in the caravan getting sorted. His uncle was off at the allotment so that helped. It was simple. Finish the hut, hop on a train to London, skip the guard for as long as he could manage, all the way if he could, jump at London Bridge during the rush hour and worry about getting past the barrier at that end when it came to it, make up some story about a broken ticket machine or something. If the worst came to the worst, just vault the barrier and run like hell. Pay for a bus and be back on the estate less than a week after he'd left. It didn't matter what Swallow said. Swallow didn't understand a thing about anything.

He packed just one bag this time. He wasn't bothered about the other stuff. He stepped out of the caravan and down the steps, pulling the door closed behind him. He felt good. He felt energised.

There was a gap in the wire fencing that was meant to keep people off the track. JB nipped through. He followed the track for the mile and a half to the station. It was the easiest way to get there and half the distance. Getting on the train was easy too. He just mingled with the crowd on the platform and looked out for the guard when he stuck his head out. When he got on he made the distance between him and the guard as big as possible.

Five people were sat in the carriage, a woman with two kids clambering over each other, another woman reading a newspaper and a fat bearded guy who kept looking at JB as if he knew the game he was playing and was ready to make a citizen's arrest. Each time JB leaned out of his seat to look down the aisle, the bearded guy planted a stare on him.

One station came and went. The guard was three carriages away. JB watched him enter the adjoining carriage, waited for as long as possible, then got up and made his way to the toilet, rocking with the motion of the train, but the woman with the newspaper got up too and started up the carriage ahead of him. She was slow and there was no way past. The fat bearded guy watched him. JB and the woman reached the end of the carriage at the same time as the guard. The guard took one look and came to a conclusion.

'Is he bothering you, love?'

'No,' said JB.

The woman shook her head and stepped into the toilet, closing the door behind her.

'You got your ticket, mate?'

'Yes thanks,' said JB.

The guard smiled and JB smiled back.

'It's in my jacket on the seat.'

'Let's see it then.'

'I'm just waiting for the toilet. I'm busting.'

'Fetch your ticket and I'll hold your place in the queue. How's that?'

JB set off back down the aisle. He could feel the guard watching him and the bearded guy too. There was no way out. Except the rolling motion had quit and the train was sending out the tell-tale squeaks and squeals that meant the driver was applying the brakes. When JB reached his seat the train was already at walking pace. Without breaking stride, without looking over his shoulder, JB grabbed his bag and continued to the end of the carriage. The door swished open.

'Oi!'

The guard was too late. JB exploded from the train. A bunch of primary kids were on the platform, all of them carrying buckets and spades and clipboards. JB barged through them, bowling one kid to the ground. Her teacher shouted after him. Beyond was the guard's voice, yelling at him to stop, but JB was too far gone already. He belted out into the station car park, got his bearings and sped down the street, already looking for somewhere to go, already thinking about getting off the street altogether, getting indoors somewhere.

There was an amusement arcade up the road and he made a beeline for it. It was dark inside and there were lads like him in there already, with their hoodies like his and jeans like his and trainers like his. It didn't matter that his said 'McKenzie' because the others said 'McKenzie' too. He made his way to the back of the place, to the darkest shadows, and then he got his breath back, always with one eye on the street, watching the traffic for a bluey, watching like a fox with the hounds after him. The more expensive bandits were back here, the ones that were 20p a throw, the ones that were meant to spit out £20 and £30. But JB knew better. They were worth it in places like Kebab Palace on the estate, places where they were on their own, because you could watch one machine and wait until it was primed to pay out. You let the casual punters stick their money in and laughed through a mouthful of meat and chips because they didn't know what they were doing, and then you struck. Once you were on the machine you stayed on until it paid out, then you left it, your stomach bursting and your pockets full. But not in places like this. In places like this they paid people to empty the machines and keep on top of things. They didn't let you hang around either. Twice already the bloke in the booth had leant back and looked at JB to see if he was spending. Now he was doing it again. JB smiled sarcastically. He found a footy game instead and dropped fifty pence in that.

He was still playing when the four lads from the beach came in. They started around the place, sticking their hands in the slots for leftover change. The bloke in the booth got on his walkie-talkie. The lads brushed past JB. The fat one stopped as if he was trying to remember and then the bloke from the booth came out.

'You lot are banned. Now scat.'

'Not us, mate. We're always in here.'

'Yeah and that's why you're banned. You never spend anything. Scat before there's trouble.'

One of the lads stepped forward.

'You threatening us?'

'I'm telling you to get out of my establishment or there'll be trouble.'

'What trouble? What are you gonna do?'

The lads were facing up to the bloke but the bloke was holding his ground. Then JB saw a fifth lad at the booth. He stuffed his hand under the counter and grabbed a bag of coins. Some of them dropped when he pulled it under the glass and the bloke heard the clatter.

'Hey!'

The lads split in all directions. JB split too. The fat one ran straight into JB and they both went over. He registered who JB was and then they were up and out on the street in the harsh light and the bloke from the booth was after them. JB shot down an alley but the fat lad carried on up the road. The bloke took after him. JB hopped over a wall and ran until his chest was bursting, ran until he found a garage block. He hid down between two garages in a place that stunk of piss and waited there, all the while thinking about the day they'd cornered him by the canal, how just as they were about to catch him he'd thought about jumping in. If he'd done it things might have turned out differently. But he hadn't jumped in. He'd made for the towpath instead.

Choices and consequences.

Night came. He'd been walking for three hours or more and he was out on the marshes. Something screeched, and he heard a haunted yelping that sounded like death. He could see the lights of the beach road way, way off in the distance. They helped to guide him. Out of nowhere came another screech, his ringtone, Carla calling him, asking where he was, asking if he was coming back and for a few minutes he was in the city with them. But it was a mess. There were voices in the background, shouting and laughter.

'Shut up, I'm talking to Jay.'

'Who's that?' JB asked.

'Just Daz and Jonno, messing about.'

'Who are they?'

'Two lads me and Missie met in town last week. They're a laugh. Missie fancies them.'

More voices.

'I don't! You do!'

'Don't listen to her . . .'

'Who's that, lover boy?'

'Look at her going red!'

'Ruined!'

'Shut up, you cow . . .'

'Carla, where's Scooby?'

'Eh?'

'Where's Scooby?'

'He's at Dicko's. They're staying in, boring farts . . .'

'Get him to call me . . .'

'All right, love. Gotta go . . .'

'See you, lover boy . . .'

'Oi, give me that phone back . . . Oi . . .'

Then they were gone and he was in the middle of nowhere again. A car appeared up ahead and started down the road towards him. JB ducked into the hedge bottom and waited for it to pass, just in case. When it had gone he concentrated his mind on the lights of the beach road and willed them closer. There were lights on the horizon, lonely ships way out at sea. JB watched one for ten minutes or more as he walked. It was sure to be moving, sure to be heading somewhere, chopping its way through the waves, but the ship didn't look like it was getting anywhere at all. When he turned his attention back to the lights of the beach road, they didn't seem to have moved either. It was like he thought he was moving when really he was standing still.

They come from the city. They come on summer weekends. They infest the place, like ants. They swarm through the middle of town in their people-carriers and sports cars and they turn the high street into a car park. They wear wrap-around sunglasses and their white teeth reflect the sunlight when they smile. They clog up the beach and say stupid things like 'The sea is disgusting,' because it doesn't look the way they'd like it to look. They fill the pavements and the galleries in the day and the restaurants in the evening and they fill both with conversations about money and property prices and then they disappear into the cottages and flats that they bought on a whim because it's the thing to do and because our town is the place to be seen.

When the weekend's over they leave their cottages and flats empty and they drive away in their people-carriers and sports cars, to return on another summer weekend and to do it all over. The town caters for their every need as if it's beholden to them and their money, and the locals admit it, they are beholden, and they smile and serve, serve and smile, but behind every local face there's anger and resentment and jealousy and it's a bitter mix that's threatening to poison the place. Everyday I feel it . . . like a pan of boiling water . . . the lid rattling . . . getting ready to blow . . .

I sound like my father.

10

The gang of lads came back. Three of them this time. JB was on the thirteenth hut. Unlucky for some.

They came sauntering along the sea wall in the afternoon. All three of them were wearing caps. Two of them, the fat lad and the little lad, had the tell-tale signs of school uniform hidden amongst their outfits: the black trousers, the white shirts. They both had white trainers on. The other had his shirt tied around his waist and was topless. He was wearing tracky bottoms with his trainers. He was either too old for school or had just not bothered going in. He had dark bruises on his face.

They were bunking off. JB knew all about it. He'd done it enough himself, just walked out of the door in his uniform, hidden it away under his hoodie, spent the days wandering around town or hanging down at the canal with whoever was up for it. That was how it started anyway. After a while he hadn't bothered to try to hide it or fool anyone. If he didn't fancy going in he just stayed in bed, told his mum it was all part of his new timetable. His mum would've gone crazy if the school had phoned to ask where he was, but the school didn't bother either and his mum was too busy with Ellie and his grandad to check up. He didn't do it every day though. Sometimes he went to school because there was nothing better to do. Sometimes he went to school to be with his mates or to surf the net on the library computers. Just because you went to school didn't mean you had to go to lessons.

JB was on his hands and knees down the side of the hut, working green paint into the wood. When the little one saw him he stopped the others and they came over.

'Oi, mate, got any fags?'

JB shook his head and carried on painting the hut. For a moment he thought the lads were going to leave it there, but they didn't. The little one pushed down between the huts, into the shadows, to get a closer look at what he was up to.

'What are you doing this for?'

JB looked up at him. He was already calculating distance and angles, in case the lad tried anything.

'It's my job,' said JB. He was surprised by that, the fact he'd called it a job. It almost stuck in his throat, because it wasn't his job, could never be his job.

'What? Painting beach huts?'

One of the other lads laughed. They were still out in the sunlight. It was difficult to see them from the dark crevice he was working in, especially now, with the little lad in between. He'd throw the tin of paint in the little one's face if he started anything. He already had the tin in his left hand. It'd be quick and simple. He'd worry about the other two after. The little lad was still asking questions though.

'You were in the arcade. You were on the footy game when it all kicked off. I knew I'd seen you before.'

JB stood up. He was bigger than the little lad, but that didn't count for much. The little ones could be the worst. They had something to prove all the time. But for now the little one wasn't looking for anything. He backed out into the sunlight and JB followed him.

'I was going home,' said JB. 'Only I didn't get there. The guard caught me without a ticket and I had to jump the train.'

'Home to where?'

'London.'

'What? You come from there?'

JB's trump card. Always. When they'd gone to Southend on the train, all of the gang together, they'd always had one over the other groups that came from this town or that town. If you were from London, and if you told people at the right moment, you could get respect just for saying it. Now it was happening again.

'So what are you down here for?'

The three lads backed away an inch. It was the tiniest thing but JB saw it. Inside he was swelling with it all, swelling with the knowledge that he had something they'd never be able to have. He went for the jugular.

'Got ASBO'd.'

'Got what?'

The topless lad piped up.

'You know what that is. Pete's brother got one for riding that motorbike he was doing up around the harbour. They made him stay in the house.'

'No,' said the fat lad. 'They told him he'd get one if he didn't stop but he never got one.'

The little one looked JB up and down.

'What you get your ASBO for?'

'Joy-riding mainly. There was some other stuff too, but it was mostly for that.'

He saw the change in them, saw it as clearly as he could see the brilliant sparkles of sunlight on the water behind them. He saw them begin to look at him in a new way, switch from being threatening to in awe of him. *He* was a joy-rider. *He* was on an ASBO. *He* was from the city. *He* was the real deal. It didn't matter that there were three of them any more and it didn't matter that they could have him if they wanted to, because they would never want to spark up trouble with somebody like this. *They* were small town. *They* were kicking paint tins and graffiti, petty vandals, mouthy in the street, lords of their estate maybe, but *they* were not what *he* was.

'Wait till Moey hears about this!' said the little lad. 'He's gonna want to meet you for sure. Are you here every day then?'

JB hid the smile that was growing behind his mouth.

'Who's Moey?' he asked.

'He's our mate. He's a real head-case. He's got an exam today.'

'I bet he's sitting there doing nothing like he did last week.'

'Yeah.'

'Why aren't you lot taking it then?'

'We've all finished. Moey's the last one. Tonight we're getting pissed down on the west beach. You should come.'

'Maybe.'

'Well, if not, come on carnival day. That's always a laugh.'

When the lads had gone, JB went back to painting the hut. Some of the care slipped away for a while and he slapped the green paint on angrily. The lads had got him thinking about the estate again. He couldn't join them on the beach. There were rules with the ASBO. He had to stay in the caravan from 7 p.m. each evening. He'd only just got away with the other day. He knew his uncle and Swallow had given him a chance. They'd let him get on the train to see if he'd go through with it or not. By sheer luck, or bad luck depending on how you looked at it, he'd ended up back at the caravan in his camp bed when he could've wound up crashing at Scooby's on the sofa. In the morning his uncle had made him breakfast and not said a word about it. When Swallow came he'd not said anything either, but JB could tell he knew the whole story. So tonight while everybody else had fun he'd sit in the caravan and try to get a picture on that crappy TV. Then, in the morning he'd be back down on the beach again. And so it would go on, for the whole summer. A long, slow, meaningless torture.

11

The sea wall and pebbles were bleached white in the sun. JB was topless, basking in it as he worked. She came out of nowhere, almost caused him to fall off the ladder when she called up to him.

'Hey!'

He thought she was one of the holiday people, come to ask him a question he couldn't answer.

'Who told you to paint these?'

With the sun shining in his face it was hard for him to see. He stood perched on the ladder, blinking, waiting for her to materialise.

'Dunno,' he said eventually.

'Somebody must have told you to do it.'

'Yeah, but he's not in charge, only in charge of me.'

'Well, that's our hut up there. Number 77.' She pointed some-where into the distance. 'And nobody told us anything about it.'

'Dunno,' he said again. 'The owners' club has something to do with it. You'd better ask them. All I know is I've got all these to paint and people come and check on me.'

'How many are there now?' she asked.

'Eighty-seven. By the time I get to the end the first one will need doing again.'

'Like that bridge,' she said.

'If you say so,' he said.

JB got a good look at her now, curled brown hair hanging in front of her eyes, legs long and tanned. She was beautiful, but she didn't look like she cared. Something pitched forwards in his stomach.

'Anyway,' he said. 'What are you doing out here?'

'I live here,' she said.

'You mean you live there,' he said.

He pointed to the town rising up behind her.

'It's all the same,' she said. 'It's the same place.'

'Not really,' he said. 'There's the town and then there's this place. I don't think they're the same. No way. Ask my uncle. He'll tell you.'

'Well, I'm telling you differently. I've lived here all my life and I should know. Anyway, it doesn't matter. I don't care what it is or whose it is. If you want to know, I'm looking for something.'

'What's that then?'

'You'll laugh,' she said.

'Promise I won't,' he said.

'It's a ships' graveyard.'

'A place where they bury ships?' he asked.

'A place where ships go to die,' she said.

She smiled. JB felt his nakedness for the first time. He wanted to put his shirt on but it was over on the wall and to climb down from the ladder and fetch it would make the act obvious. He carried on painting instead, letting the brush sweep over the wood, letting the paint seep into the cracks, running the brush forward and backward, expertly.

'What's your name?' she said.

'They call me JB.'

'Can I call you JB too?'

'Up to you,' he said.

'Do you have another name?'

JB shook his head.

'I'll see you around, JB,' she said.

She stepped on to the pebbles and started away from him.

'What's your name?' he asked.

But she didn't look back.

'Hang on,' he shouted.

But she was already five huts away from him, her feet making crunching sounds on the pebbles. He thought about jumping down off the ladder and running after her, but he didn't. He watched her go until she was just a speck in the distance, melting into the heat haze. He'd only ever seen a thing like that over the car park back home, and once down at the canal when Scooby had pitched a Smirnoff Ice bottle up the path to see if it disappeared into it. He'd not seen it in a place so open before, not seen it melt the horizon and take someone away from him. He stared for an age, his jaw hanging open. Then he went back to painting the hut, his strokes long and powerful, the paint even and easy, like the brush and the arm extending from it were all part of one conjoined machine.

Emma says she saw it last summer. I remember the night she phoned to tell me all about it. She said her and Steve took the motor boat out in the evening and set off up the coast past the holiday village, right up into the channel where the reserve is. They grounded the boat on the beach there and built a fire. I told her she was crazy because the wardens might have seen the smoke and gone berserk but she said it was a Sunday and there were no wardens around. She said that when the sun was setting Steve got all nervous about getting the boat in before dark so they put out the fire and started back. The next thing she knew they were right in the middle of it.

It started when they spotted a mast rising up out of the water. Emma wanted to ignore it but Steve said he had to look closer because he'd never seen it before and then she said it all went really strange. She said when they turned the boat towards the shore there were suddenly masts everywhere, a drowned forest. When they got up close to the beach there were dozens of ships there, some really, really old, their frames rotten and black. She said there was a mist that made it difficult to see. After a few minutes she freaked out and told Steve to take her home but Steve had trouble turning the boat in the right direction. She said they spent a few minutes going round and round in circles. The boat was bumping against things under the water. She started to panic, even though it was just bits of old boats. Eventually the mist cleared and Steve got them back in open water. When they looked back they couldn't see the masts anywhere. I told her she'd been smoking something but she swore she hadn't. Thing is I know Steve so it was definitely a possibility. But every time I talked to her about it the story was exactly the same so I started to believe her and do some research.

Turns out she's not the first. Turns out that loads of people reckon they've seen the place. There are loads of websites about it. I was going to ask Dad but what's the point? I know he doesn't believe it and I know why. It's because he hasn't seen it for himself. He'd say that as he knows the channel like the back of his hand, and has never seen it or heard of it from anybody except crackpots and fairy-headed people like Emma, he's got no reason to believe it.

12

Carnival.

His uncle told him to take a rest. It was all agreed, as long as he was back in the caravan by seven. He started for town, not really knowing where he was heading, just walking in the direction of the buildings, sometimes on the sea wall, sometimes on the beach, always looking out for something to happen, nerves sharp, muscles tense.

The beach grew busier as he got closer to the town. Kids and parents on bikes, kids clambering on the breakers, a crowd of people outside the pub on the front, beer glasses full, laughter drifting down to him at the surf line where he walked, keeping his head down, keeping his distance.

They said they'd be at the monument, but he didn't know where the monument was. The town was bursting with cars and pedestrians and people trying to clear the street for the parade. Three times he had to walk into the road to get past people. A car hooted at him and somebody called him a 'silly little prick' but he kept his head down and his hoodie up and didn't look back to see.

He found the monument in a courtyard open to the High Street. They were sat on the steps, a gang of eight or nine. Two were girls. JB hesitated, but it was too late. The fat lad was calling him over.

'Hey! Hey!'

Heads turned and eyes fixed on him. The little lad was there and the lad with the bruises. Somewhere far off was a drumming sound, the approach of the parade.

'Moey, look, it's JB. I told you he'd come down.'

Moey was on the top step. He had his arm around a girl with streaked blonde hair and he was drinking a Red Bull. He pushed the can into the girl's hands and some of it spilled on her white leggings. She swore and started wiping at the stain. He laughed and hopped down. JB recognised him. He'd been in the arcade with the rest of them. He was the one who'd stolen the money from the cash desk. He had eyes that looked like they were somewhere else. He sauntered over to JB and then at the last second jabbed a punch at JB's face. JB moved instinctively, ducking back and left away from it. Moey shouted.

'Yaaahhhhhhhhhhh!'

Again JB stood there. Across the road two or three people stopped to see what was going on.

'Boxer!'

'Not any more,' said JB.

'Once a boxer always a boxer. Ain't that right?'

The lad with the bruises nodded. Some girl came up to him and started biting his neck. She had a halter top on and JB saw the ring in her belly button. The lad with the bruises turned his attention on her and tickled her until she screamed.

'Get off. Get offfffffffff!'

More looks from the people across the road. One of them shouted something. Moey turned. JB took a look at him. Moey lifted his right hand to his face to block out the sunlight. His knuckles were red and full of scars and scabs, his thumb and forefinger stained yellow-brown.

'Piss off!' he yelled.

There were four or five people opposite, all over sixty. They were waiting in the shade for the carnival parade to pass. JB dropped his head, the automatic reflex. The sound of the drums was louder now. He could hear the majorettes, too. The fat lad clambered up the monument and called after him. JB got to the third step where the girl was still wiping at her leggings. She turned her eyes up at his for a second, saw he was looking and went back to her problem. JB climbed to the fourth step and looked back over the heads of the others.

'Moey's mad,' said the fat lad. 'Hey, Moey,' he shouted. 'Tell him about the time you stuck that frog in your mouth and scared that woman to death!'

Moey shook his head and waved his arms.

'You tell him. It's no big deal.'

'Priceless,' said the fat lad and he laughed to himself.

The parade came up the high street. It started with a marching band. Moey marched around on the pavement under the monument, pretending to blow a trumpet and everybody laughed except the girl with the stain who was still busy with her leggings. A float came next, made up to look like a pirate ship. Long John Silver or somebody was on top of it, waving. Two more floats passed. The second one was carrying the Carnival Queen and Princesses.

'She's such a slag,' said the girl with the stain.

'Her sister's worse,' said the girl with the belly-button piercing. 'You should have gone for it, girl.'

'Jog on,' said the girl with the stain. 'I wouldn't be seen dead on that thing!'

The Carnival Queen saw the girls on the monument and deliberately looked the other way. Another marching band arrived. This time it was made up of lads and girls. Moey ran into the road and marched alongside them.

'Hey, look at Moey,' said the fat lad. 'What a tosser!'

'I'll tell him you said that,' said the girl with the piercing. The fat lad's smile dropped a notch.

Moey marched on down the road. Behind the band came another float. It was made to look like a lifeboat but it was patched up with bits of wood and tape and bandages. On the side was a sign that read: 'Support your local lifeboat!'

The blokes on the boat were dressed in the same way, as a lifeboat crew, but with deflated and torn lifejackets. One of them was only wearing a pair of armbands, some swimming trunks and goggles. He was a big man with broad shoulders. He was laughing and joking with the crowd and then he saw Moey messing with the parade and his face turned to thunder.

He was down off the float in an instant and his voice overpowered the band when he shouted.

'Get away, you stupid fool! Get off the bloody road. You're a bloody disgrace.'

Moey darted back towards the monument as the big man came at him. More people were watching now. The band marched on and the float stopped short so that the event took centre stage. For the first time, the big man saw the group of teenagers on the monument, drink cans scattered on the steps, crisp packets and sweet wrappers, plastic bags strewn about.

'You can get down from there, too. Where's your bloody respect? Who do you think you are? This is a family day, not another thing for you lot to destroy.'

JB got around the back of the monument and jumped down. He still had his hoodie up and he was glad of it. He hadn't taken any notice of the monument, hadn't even thought about it. He took a closer look now. He could see the bronze boat on the top and the names of the men on the plaque, the word 'tragedy' and a date, '1968'.

Now that the big man was involved, one of the oldies came over the road and started up too.

'You should have heard them,' he said. 'You should have heard the way they spoke to us.'

'It doesn't surprise me, Albert,' said the big man. 'It's the way they are these days. Now bugger off, the lot of you. This is your town's big day and all you can think to do is spoil it. Go on! Go!'

'What are we spoiling?' shouted the girl with the piercing. 'Just sitting here . . .' Her voice was high-pitched, shrill.

'Don't shout at me, you silly little girl,' said the big man. 'Get down off there and take your rubbish with you.'

Some of the gang had already started to slip away into the alley behind the monument. The fat lad had gone for a start, the little lad too. Both the girls were just about there, standing with two of the lads JB hadn't seen before. JB was next, half-way between the alley and Moey and the lad with the bruises. He was ready to go but Moey wasn't finished and JB wanted to see what was going to happen next.

'What? What? What?'

Moey kept saying it, over and over, swinging his arms from in to out, gesturing innocence and defiance.

'What are you gonna do? Come on then!'

He shouted the last three words but was taking backward steps as he did. The big man wasn't to be messed with. Seeing two more of the lads off, he turned to JB.

'You too. Go on. Don't hang around here with your bad smell.'

JB stood his ground until Moey and the lad with the bruises reached him. Moey put one arm across JB's shoulder and one arm over the shoulder of the lad with the bruises. After a moment he pulled JB's hoodie off.

'It's too easy with the thing on,' he said.

JB grabbed the hood back, thought about pulling it on again, realised this was a test he had to pass if Moey was going to take him seriously.

They faced up to the big man for three more seconds, the big man staring them down, the lads making their stand, until Moey turned to JB.

'Come on,' he said. 'It's not worth it.'

They went into the alley and JB followed.

'Tosser!'

Moey shouted it as loud as he could and then they legged it.

They darted through the alleyways, around the backs of the buildings and came out at a row of shops. The fat lad went in and ten seconds later the two other lads followed. When they came out again they had four packs of bangers.

They walked up the high street to the park. The parade was ahead of them now, the street littered with confetti and streamers, cars back on the road, busy again. The cars ran over the coloured streamers, mashing them into dark, tattered strips.

JB went with them to the harbour. The parade and its people had come to a halt on the grass slopes above the west beach so the harbour was quiet. The tide was out and the water had drained at the edges.

There was just a dirty brown pool of sea water in the middle of the black mud where the harbour trough was deepest, the smell of fish, the smell of the black sludge. The fat lad pulled a banger from his pocket and lit it.

'Listen to this,' he said.

He tossed the banger towards the water. It landed on the mud before going off. There was the slightest fizz and then it sat there lifeless. They all laughed and called him a fat tosser. Even JB. The fat lad laughed too, at himself, but his cheeks were puffed and pink with the frustration of it. He set about repeating the process, trying to save himself, but Moey was having none of it.

'Oi, give us it here,' he said. 'Let me show you how it's done.'

He grabbed the banger from the fat lad's fingers and lit it with his own lighter. Then he stood with it in his fist. The fat lad shifted nervously.

'Throw it then . . .'

But Moey held on to the banger. He lifted it up before those vacant eyes until it was an inch from his own nose.

'Moey, get rid of it . . .'

The fat lad started to inch backwards and the others did the same. JB moved too. Moey smiled and threw the banger in the air. It sailed in an arc across the mud, was a foot above the water when it exploded. The sound pummelled the harbour walls and rebounded back like cannon fire. A flock of seagulls took to the air, squawking wildly, and the sound followed them up into the air in the direction of the slopes.

Now the others tried it, one at a time, each of them pushing the boundary between lighting the banger and throwing it, but none of them could match Moey, none of them dared. Even the lad with the bruises didn't have the nerve. When it was JB's turn he lit the banger and watched it burn while the gang watched him.

One second.

Two.

Three.

How long had Moey held it for? Five? Six seconds? How many tests would there be? JB held on for one more second, got to four and then threw. The banger travelled in the air for the briefest of moments, not even reaching the harbour wall before it exploded, scattering the gang again, causing them to grab their ears, the fat lad hollering at the top of his lungs.

'Whoah . . . talk about cutting it fine . . .'

'Short fuse! Moey, what if that was yours?'

'Nah, I sensed it . . . just like he sensed it. Boxers see . . .'

JB hadn't sensed anything. He stood there looking at the spent banger on the floor, trying to hold his nerve, but inside he was shaking and his heart was racing at a hundred miles per hour. The girl with the stain came over to him.

'You're mad, you are,' she said.

JB shrugged.

'What's your name again?'

'JB.'

'I'm Lisette. Is it true you're from London?'

'Yeah.'

'What's it like there?'

'It's all right,' he said.

'Better than this boring dump, I'll bet.'

Moey came up behind Lisette and wrapped his arms around her. She leaned back into him. He was about to speak when three men came around the corner.

'I knew it'd be you lot!'

The big man from the parade was in front, two more of the men from the same float behind. The gang split in all directions, charging along the harbour wall and disappearing into the gaps between the oyster sheds. Only JB was left, not sure which way to run, not sure about any of it.

'You again. I don't know you, do I?'

JB split too. He ran after Moey and Lisette. They crossed the road in between the traffic and ducked down into another alley. He followed behind. The smell of chips wafted up over a stone wall and when JB stopped for breath he saw that they were behind the fish-and-chip shop on the High Street.

'What's his problem?' said JB.

'He's got it in for us,' said Lisette. 'He's always doing it. He reckons we're banned from the harbour but we're not. He can't ban anybody from anywhere.'

'Thinks he's God,' said Moey.

JB looked back up the alley. The fat lad was hiding at the far end, peering around the corner in the direction of the harbour. When JB turned back Moey had Lisette against the wall, kissing her. Lisette pushed him off. Her eyes met JB's for a second and Moey saw. Moey leant back against the wall and took a packet out of his pocket.

'Hey,' he said to JB. 'Want to buy some of this?'

'Nah, got no money,' said JB.

'Have an eighth. I'll give you it for twenty quid.'

JB shook his head.

'What's up? Has the big shot from London gone soft?'

'Serious. I'm skint.'

'Okay then, ten quid.'

'Leave it,' said Lisette. 'If he doesn't want any that's up to him.'

'Why do you care so much?' said Moey.

'I don't,' said Lisette. 'I'm just saying.'

'Well, it's got nothing to do with you. This is between me and JB.'

Moey turned to JB again. Those vacant eyes were changing, showing something darker. JB shifted.

'Have you already got a stash? Is that it?'

'Nah.'

'Take some on credit then. You can owe me.'

JB didn't want it but Moey was getting difficult and he didn't want that either. He reached out and took the gear and stuffed it in his pocket.

'I've got to get back,' he said.

He left them in the alley. When he got to the High Street he looked behind him. Moey had Lisette pressed against the wall again. The fat lad was approaching from the other end but when he saw Moey and Lisette he stopped. He lifted an arm to JB and JB lifted an arm back. JB ran across the High Street and on to the beach, making his way back to the site. He could see the huts in the distance. He thought about spending a day painting beach huts and nothing else. He took the gear from his pocket and weighed it in his hands. He was going to throw it into the sea, went through all the motions to do so, and then stopped. Scooby would think he was mad but Scooby couldn't even sleep without it any more, and that was why he wanted to get rid of it, because it wasn't him and he hated what it did to Scooby, the way it made him so distant it was impossible to reach him, but he wanted to keep it too, just in case there was a night where he might need it and welcome it. He knew that day was coming. He didn't know when but the day was surely coming because days like it always came.

Emma worked at the hotel on the front last summer and I went a few times. It's four-star and whenever anybody famous comes to town they stay there. Last year there was a TV chef and an actor off East-enders. This hotel has fancy linen tablecloths and plush carpets and all the bedrooms are en suite and you think you're in some other world until you take a closer look and then you see the stains where they've washed stuff out of the carpets and the marks on the walls and the scuffs on the skirting boards. And all of the staff are like Emma, seventeen and getting next to nothing. Emma says they get all the crappy jobs like cleaning under the beds and she's always on about how she does the job half-heartedly so they say it's this posh place but it's not, it's just a trick, an illusion, and people pay all this money to stay there and somebody gets rich from it but it's not the people who work there and it's not the manager either. And the worst thing about it? When I went there and walked in, when all the people looked at me, I was embarrassed to be myself. These people, staring from behind their wine glasses, looking down their noses, making eyes at each other. I should have screamed the place down, knocked some of those noses out of shape. But I didn't do anything. I spotted Emma and raced in her direction, feeling their eyes at my back, wanting to disappear, like a maidservant stepping out of the scullery in front of the Queen.

13

'It was Scooby's idea. We were down at the kiddies' playground on the swings. Scooby was messing with the little ones, you know where they have the bar across the front to stop kids falling out. He was doing that thing where you try and get the swing to go over the top, so the chain wraps up, then he was clambering up the pole and unravelling it before starting again. We were all watching him do it. There was nothing else to do.'

JB turned his attention away from the painting and squinted in the direction of Swallow. Swallow was stirring the next tin, trying to do it without getting any of the paint on his clothes.

'How's that?' Swallow asked, tipping the tin in JB's direction.

'About right,' said JB. 'One more minute. Anyway, this bloke pulls up in a clapped-out Metro and starts giving us all this about it stopping his kids playing there, but it was dark already and we never went down there in the day so he was talking rubbish. Scooby goes over to him and tells him where to go and they start pushing and shoving each other. Carla starts screaming at Scooby and keeps grabbing him but he just keeps pushing her away. This guy tries to get Scooby in a headlock but Scooby rolls him over. I was gonna jump in but Scooby was doing all right. He was landing a few punches and that. Anyway, after a bit the guy gets up and runs inside. I think he thought he was gonna get a kicking, which he would have if we'd piled in, but Scooby can handle himself so it didn't matter. He might have got a kicking from Scooby anyway. We were all laughing and that and then Scooby notices the guy's dropped his car keys. Quick as a flash he starts running to the car. We all chase after him to see what he's gonna do. I didn't know he was gonna get in the thing. I didn't know he was gonna drive it. When he opened it up I just got in with him for a laugh. I wasn't thinking. I was just going along with it all. Next thing I know Scooby's got the engine running and we're racing around the car park. I told him to quit but I was laughing and he didn't listen to me. He turns the radio on and cranks it up as loud as it goes. Carla and the rest are watching us and doing the same, laughing at Scooby but trying to get him to stop. Then the guy comes back down to the car park and, just like that, Scooby takes off down the road. It was okay in the car park, just a game really, but when he pulled out on to the road and there were other cars there, that got me. I started shouting at him to pull over but he wouldn't. He just kept shouting back that it was only for a bit. We drove down to the outlet centre and went into the car park there. I thought he was gonna pull in and we could get out and there'd be no harm done, and at least we were off the road, but he started racing around there, skidding everywhere, getting the tyres smoking. Suddenly I saw the blueys. I turned the radio off and told him we had to get out. As soon as he stopped the car I was out of there. The blueys were just behind, two cars. When they got out, two went after me and two after Scooby. Scooby ran off in one direction and I went the other. I ended up down on the canal towpath. I was gasping but I thought I'd lost them. I hid under the bridge for a bit behind a concrete thing and then I started to make my way back to the estate. I thought if I could make it there I'd be safe. They wouldn't know it like I did, all the alleys and gardens you can jump, but I should have stayed put for longer. As soon as I came out from under the bridge I saw two of them up ahead on the towpath and they saw me. I turned and ran the other way and the other two were down there. Scooby had got away and they had me trapped instead. I went for it but they grabbed me. That was it. I got the blame for it all. The guy didn't even make any charges against Scooby for the fight. It was just me. I got blamed for the car and everything even though they knew it wasn't me driving. They just said it didn't matter. They wanted me to grass Scooby up but you don't do that, do you? You don't grass up your mates.'

'Well, that depends.'

'On what?'

'What about Scooby? You protected him but he didn't protect you. He didn't tell them it was his fault.'

'It doesn't work like that. If you get caught you take the rap for it.'

'So you get the ASBO and you get sent away and Scooby carries on as if nothing happened. Jay, this is your life we're talking about. When you want to get a job and you've got this hanging around your neck do you think they're going to care about your loyalty to some mate?'

'He's not just some mate.'

'I'm not saying you two aren't close. I'm saying there's a limit. You know they could have put you away anyway, just for being sat in that seat.'

'No limits. That's what real friends are about.'

'If there are no limits, Scooby should have gone to the police station and admitted he was driving the car and you were telling him to stop.'

'Yeah? Well, like I told you, it doesn't work like that.'

'In the real world it does.'

'That was the real world, not this place. That's your problem. That's what you don't get. I know what the real world is. You don't. You're the same as the rest of 'em, talking like you understand when you understand nothing.'

'Jay, I understand.'

'You don't understand. Nobody understands except me. It's my life. I understand it.'

What he wanted was to throw the tin of paint at Swallow and run. Run and run until his lungs gave out. But there was nowhere to run to, not really. He was an animal in a cage, forced to go through the same routine each and every day, beach hut, beach hut, beach hut, nothing changing, nothing threatening to change, while people like Swallow came to look at him and prod him for stuff and try to tell him they knew when they didn't know a thing.

He's painting beach huts. There's something about him. He's got amazing skin and shoulders. He's not from around here.

I told him about the ship's graveyard and he looked at me like I was mad! I had to walk off because I was so embarrassed. Some old guy down on the beach told me that it's there for sure, but that I'll never find it when I'm looking for it. But I'm going to keep looking for it anyway. Sometimes if you look for things and don't find what you're looking for you end up finding something else instead. Something better even.

14

'I'm sending you away,' she said. 'You heard them. This ASBO thing. What chance have I got of stopping you breaking it? Not a hope. You could have killed somebody. You could have killed yourself. I'm not letting you kill yourself. I'm sending you over the water, to your uncle.'

He was dreaming again, but he didn't know it. If he'd been able to climb out of himself and watch the boy that was sleeping, he'd have seen the sweat on his forehead and heard the sounds that came from deep in his being, the desperation rising up like dark water.

'We went there when you were younger. Remember?'

He shook his head.

'Yes, you do,' she said. 'He lives by the sea. We used to visit him on the train, spend the whole day there, eat chips on the beach.'

'Oh, yeah. He's a fisherman.'

'Not any more. He's a caretaker or something. He's got work for you. The services think it's a good idea. It'll give you some direction. They're going to monitor you. There's a new programme for families like us, a chance to make a new start. I might be able to get housing down there. Imagine it, living by the sea, a real house, a garden even.

Your sister shouldn't have to grow up around here. You shouldn't have to grow up around here.'

'You grew up here . . .'

'And look at the mess I'm in. Anyway, things have changed. This place has changed. I don't like what you're becoming, Jay. I'm getting you out of here. I'm not watching my only son go the same way as his father.'

'I'm not going.'

'It's what your grandad wanted.'

'Yeah, well, he's dead.'

She slapped him then, hard, across the face. It was something she'd never done before. She'd pushed and pinched before, and hit his arms while he fended her off, but those times had been born of frustration and hardly mattered. He'd mostly laughed at her. The slap was different. It was real. He didn't know what to do about it except hide the pain he was feeling and pretend it was nothing. His cheek was stinging as though he'd fallen into a thousand nettles and in that moment something changed between them.

When he woke the sweat was real. The feeling of desperation was real, too. Somehow he could feel the pain in his cheek, a searing red heat that he didn't understand. He lay in the bed staring at the roof of the caravan, recalling that night again, the hollow feeling in his stomach that told him she meant it and that it really was going to happen.

He'd shouted at her. He didn't know what else to do. Told her he wasn't going anywhere and that he didn't care about the ASBO or the courts or the social services or even her. He told her he'd go to prison, that it didn't bother him, and then Ellie had appeared in the doorway. She was rubbing her eyes from sleep. When he saw her he stopped shouting. His mother had grabbed her and taken her back to bed, leaving him there in the middle of the living room, staring after the two of them, a lost child. He might have been ten years old again, wanting his mother to make everything better. He might have been but he wasn't. He was sixteen and his future was shot to pieces.

My favourite place around here is the reserve. None of the outsiders ever get that far and none of the locals are bothered about it being there. Once I pass beyond the headland and the town slips out of view it's just me and my thoughts. There's a 'Keep Out' sign but I'm not doing any harm, just walking and thinking. I watch my step and I stay clear of the birds. I'm getting to know them, Oystercatchers and Turnstones, Redshanks with their red legs showing. There are Marsh Harriers too. I've seen them flying low over the reed beds, watched them drop down on their prey. I'm learning the names of the plants and flowers too, like Sea Lavender and Wild Carrot. In one direction the mud flats go on forever to the sea. In the other direction the marshes sit silent and solemn. On a quiet evening out there when the water is still, a person can become nothing, nothing at all, and that's the best feeling in the world.

15

Her name was Sal. She appeared like a mirage, out of the heat haze, her long hair sprawling and falling in front of her eyes, hiding her beauty and adding to it at the same time. He got down off the ladder and waited for her to reach him.

'Looking for that graveyard again?'

'Nope, just wandering aimlessly.'

She hopped on to the sea wall and sat down, leaning back with her arms behind her, turning her face to the sunlight, closing her eyes. She had a halter top on and a tiny pair of denim shorts. Her long legs were stretched out in front of her. She had perfect white trainers on. He felt unclean standing there in his shorts that were splashed with paint.

'You're so lucky, being out here every day.'

'Right,' he said. 'It's what I always dreamed of.'

'There's worse things. You're out in the sun. Your own boss . . .'

'Except most people get paid for being their own boss.'

'You don't get paid?'

'Are you kidding?'

'So why are you doing it?'

JB stood over her. She still had her eyes closed. There was a difference this time. It wasn't like with the lads. It was about telling her the truth or a lie. She knew nothing about him. He could be anything, say anything and she wouldn't know. As long as she kept her eyes shut and didn't look at him. But he felt something, something he hadn't felt before. It was nestled deep inside and it was telling him he could not lie, that lying would be a mistake. No, it wasn't just that. It was more to do with not wanting to lie, not wanting to pretend. But the truth? He couldn't just tell her the truth.

'Don't you have a job?' he asked.

She opened her eyes. For a second or two she looked straight at him, as though she were searching for something in him, then she put a hand over her face to block the sun and he couldn't see her eyes any more.

'I should get one really,' she said. 'I worked the last three summers in the ice-cream stall on the west beach, but I told them I'm not doing it this year. Standing there scooping ice-cream all day for £3 an hour. I mean that's all right when you're fourteen but . . .'

'Three quid!'

'I know, it's a joke. My dad thinks it's the best job in the world, though. He knows the guy that owns the stall. He's angry at me for letting his mate down. Can you believe it?'

'How old are you, then?'

'Seventeen. I finish sixth form next week. I've got one exam to go. What about you?'

'I'm through with exams, through with school . . .'

'No, how old?'

'Yeah, seventeen, same as you.'

The lie came, escaped before he could stop it. But it was just a small one. He'd be seventeen soon enough. Give or take a few months he was already seventeen. Older even.

'When's your birthday then?'

'When's yours?'

'I asked first.'

She was smiling now, sitting up suddenly, active in the game. He held the paintbrush between them.

'Don't get violent,' she said. 'Mine's in August. The curse of being the youngest in my year at school.'

'January,' he said.

'Right. So you'd be in the year above, if you were still at school that is . . .'

'I don't want to think about school.'

'Me neither. Just because I'm still there doesn't mean I want to be.'

'Why are you then?'

'My dad mostly. But I'm putting my foot down, teaching him a few lessons. What's your dad reckon to you doing this then?'

JB lowered the brush into the paint, worked the bristles into it, lifted it out and continued with the job.

'I have to get on with this,' he said. 'The brush is going dry. It's impossible when the brush goes dry.'

She watched him for a minute or more without saying anything, then she said,

'That's okay. I'm just going to stay here in the sun.'

'If you insist,' he said.

'One more thing.'

'What's that?'

'Why do you call yourself JB?'

He shrugged.

'Nobody uses their real name in the city. You don't use your real name unless you have to.'

'Why not?'

'Dunno.'

'I use my own name. I can say it too. Sal Jefferies. Easy.'

'Yeah, but it's different here.'

'Why?'

'You can just be yourself if you live here and nobody cares. That's the difference between here and there . . . or one of the differences . . .'

'You should try living where everybody knows you. It's not so easy. What other differences are there?'

'Are you kidding?'

'No . . .'

He opened his mouth to speak but nothing came out. Instead he watched her as she closed her eyes again and lay back on the wall, watched her lift her knees so her legs were up, her arms bent at the elbows, her fingers locked behind her head. He studied her shape. He felt as though he could watch her forever and never get bored of it.

16

He thought about her all evening, sat for a while under the tree in the caravan park, turning his mobile in his fingers, wondering if she'd text like she said she would. He took the pen-knife out of his pocket and scraped at the dirt with it, scraped the word 'Sal'. After leaving it a minute he scuffed it out with his trainer. He scraped 'Carla' instead then scuffed that out, too. Finally he scraped 'JB' and left it there. He grabbed a stone and ran it along the knife blade, sharpening the blade for fun. He pressed his thumb against the blade to see how sharp he could get it. He sat there while the heat drained from the day. He couldn't bring himself to do anything else. It was like a part of him had suddenly gone missing, an emptiness inside. But it was also fullness, a feeling of carrying something around, something that needed looking after and caring for. He wasn't sure what to make of it all. Later, when his uncle disappeared off to the allotments, he sat in the caravan with the portable TV on, not really watching it, not caring what was happening, just sitting there watching the characters on the screen, hardly hearing the things that were said between them, thinking only of what Sal had said, over and over and over again, and still there was no message, just the blinking of the signal light.

Later still, with his uncle snoring away in the back, the dog sighing and shifting position in his basket, he lay with his eyes open, looking out of the curtains at the stars. He hadn't thought about the estate all day. He hadn't thought about Carla or any of them. He felt bad about it and tried to think about them instead, but each time he did Sal came back and forced her way in. He reached under the bed and felt for the packet of dope, rolled a spliff in the darkness and then stopped, thinking about his uncle, thinking about the ASBO. He opened the window above the bed and leaned out of it, feeling the cool air on his face. He grabbed his lighter and lit the spliff, sucked in a lungful and held it there. He closed his eyes. He looked out at the blackness of the marshes and waited for the familiar lightness to come and then he let himself delve through the thoughts in his head, delve gently without order, without restriction, delve with a warmth that softened and shaped and massaged all that was happening in his life, not making things better, not making things worse, just changing his perspective until sleep swallowed him.

In his dream he was six years old. Dawn was breaking through the curtains and he could hear the rush of traffic that meant the city was waking. He was lying in his bed in the flat, staring up at the pictures of dinosaurs on the wallpaper, imagining himself as a time traveller sent to investigate the past. The rest of the dream came in fragments, each one a photograph, the sound of heavy footsteps on the stairs, approaching like thunder, coming close, closer still. A hammering at the door. Men shouting. The sound of his mother in the next room. His father rushing past the doorway. The hammering louder and louder. His mother screaming. In they came, one after another. He could see their uniforms flashing past the doorway. Now his father was shouting, sounding scared, sounding in pain. One of them came into the room, looked at him for a second, then turned back and closed the door behind him. Thirty seconds later his father was gone.

But some of the men stayed and they turned the place over. They came into his room, went through his wardrobe, his clothes, his toys and games. When they left the flat was a mess. His mother was a mess. Everything was a mess.

In his dream he was a little lost boy. The marshes were still. He could hear them breathing, hear the sea washing over the pebbles on the beach, hear the calls of the night. He was naked but it didn't matter. Out on the marshes in the darkness there was nobody to see his nakedness. Still he felt afraid. And cold. His feet were wet, sinking slowly into soft mud. Tall grasses were tickling the backs of his legs. Though it was dark, insects were at his soft skin. He itched from head to toe. He could see the lights of the caravan park and he desperately wanted to reach them but each time he tried to move he felt his feet sink deeper, the mud swallowing and digesting him little by little, so that it was up to his knees now. He could feel a growing panic inside. He had to move. If he stayed still he would die. That was the simple nature of it. But when he tried to move he could no longer lift his legs from the mud. It was up to his thighs already. Panic took over. He fought with all his strength, fought to drag himself free but it was no use. All he succeeded in doing was overbalancing. He fell on his back. Above him, the stars were shining down, so many stars. He had never seen a sky like this before, so clear, so full of possibility, and he would never see another because the mud was around his ears already. There was a popping sound and the sound of the sea and then the sound of the sea disappeared, was replaced instead with a dead rush that held his own pounding heartbeat within it. He screamed, screamed at the top of his lungs, but nobody came to help him and the final time he opened his mouth the mud poured in, filled it, ran into the spaces behind his lips and then down his throat until all he could see and feel and hear was the terrible blackness consuming him . . .

He woke sweating and painfully gasping for air. His fingers were locked tight on the duvet and he had to think about how to use them before he could free the duvet from his grip. His toes seemed to be locked in place too, as though he'd suffered some sort of seizure. It frightened him. For a moment he lay there trying to make sense of it all, then the first memory of the nightmare came back to him and he started to relax. Anybody could have a nightmare. They just came at you unexpectedly. He rolled over on to his side, to find the dog sitting there looking back at him. He could hear the steady thump, thump, thump of the dog's tail on the linoleum. He reached out an arm and stroked the dog's head, taking comfort from its company.

When he looked at his mobile the little green light was flashing a message. His heart skipped. It was a message from Sal.

'Had a gd day. Sal x'

It was nothing really, but in truth it was everything.

17

'What is that? A poem?'

'A poem! You're having a laugh. It's lyrics.'

'Let's see then.'

'No, I was just messing about.'

'Let me read it.'

'You won't like it.'

'That's for me to decide.'

'You can read one.'

As soon as he gave her the book he jumped down on to the beach and put some distance between them. He picked up a pebble, threw it, tried to reach the sea with it, but it came up short and scattered the smaller stones at the tide line. After a minute he came back up the beach and vaulted up on to the wall. She was staring at the page.

This isolation
Is your creation
This desperation
Your legislation

This population
Suffering suffocation
Alienation
Discrimination
Assassination
Termination

He waited until her eyes lifted back to his.

'You wrote this?'

'Most of it. Me and Dic . . . me and my mate did it. Used a rhyming dictionary off the Net in the school library. There's no way I'd remember all those words.'

'Sing it then.'

'You don't sing it. You say it.'

'So say it.'

He shook his head.

'I just write them down.'

'Is it about you?'

He shrugged.

'So what does alienation mean?' she asked.

'Why, is it wrong?'

'No.'

'If you know why are you asking?'

'I was just joking. Sorry. I think it's brilliant. Emma's boyfriend should read it. He's in a band. They write crappy lyrics.'

Early evening was his time, a space between the painting job and his curfew hours. The sea was calm, lapping at the shoreline, and she'd come to find him, just like she said she would. They set off back towards the town following the sea wall.

'What does your dad do?' he asked.

'He's a carpenter, but he works the lifeboat too.'

She stopped for a second, stared hard at the water.

'He mostly builds fences and sheds. He made a lot of money on the beach huts. He built most of the ones on the front. There was a real boom for them. Do you know how much they go for?'

'How much?'

'Last count was £12,000.'

'For one beach hut?'

'Well, that one had running water. Most of them go for about £6,000.'

'Maybe I'll build one and sell it.'

'They wouldn't let you. The council control all that. There's a waiting list and everything.'

He laughed.

'I wouldn't have a clue anyway.'

'So what's with the music?'

'Nothing really. Back at school a few of us got together and set up a recording studio. Really basic. Just some mixing decks and that. It was all right for a while, until the music teacher left. Someone nicked the new teacher's mobile and nobody owned up so she stopped letting us go in there when she wasn't about. We quit after that.'

'You should meet Emma. She's into her music.'

'What about you?'

'I'm not bothered what I listen to.'

'I mean what are you in to?'

'Nothing really. I just want to travel and see the world. Can't go for at least a year though. I'm saving for one of those tickets where you get five flights. You can go anywhere.'

He looked at her.

'Maybe one day,' he said. 'When I win the lottery . . .'

'Do you do it?'

'Nah. Mostly I get credit for this.'

He held up his phone.

'You got some then,' she said. 'You could've texted me last night.'

'Got it this morning off Baz. He's sound.'

They cut into an alleyway. It ran up the side of the hill between the houses with the driveways that JB had seen on the first day. There was a meadow there with horses. She stopped. A grey horse came forward to meet her. A black horse did the opposite though, stepped back into the field to keep its distance.

'They've been here ages,' she said. 'The black one doesn't like people. I think it was mistreated before it came here.'

And then she said, 'Do you want to go?'

'No,' said JB. 'I'll walk back with you.'

'Okay,' she said.

He walked her up the hill. Her house was massive, with huge windows in the front that looked out over the town and the sea. The front door was big and heavy like the door to the courts where they'd slapped the ASBO on him. He felt foolish standing there and even though she said she'd see him the next day and even though she waited a second longer than she needed to before she started up the path, he knew the gap between them was too vast. It was only a matter of time before she woke up to it.

18

It was before nine but already the sun had real warmth to it. He knew something was wrong the moment he reached the bank of sea grass behind the huts. One of the dog walkers he saw morning after morning, one who had got to saying hello, gave him a look instead. As he stepped down on to the walkway the look started to take on meaning.

The storage shed was open.

JB stepped up to it. The lock had been torn away from the wood. One side of it was lying on the floor down the side of the hut, the other hanging loosely from the splintered door. There were paint tins lying in the entrance. One tin had come open and spilled yellow paint. The paint had settled in the night so that the whole of the bottom of the hut was covered. It had seeped between all of the other paint tins on the floor creating a carpet of yellow. JB reached down and pressed a finger into it.

A rage started to build inside him. It was swimming around in his stomach already, looking for an escape. His breathing was shallow. His chest felt tight. He stepped back from the hut and surveyed the line of huts, thirty-three of them, freshly painted, the rest of the line stretching away, anticipating their revival . . . except somebody had been at them. Scattered at random points up the line were more tins of paint.

There was writing on the huts he'd already painted. The writing was in big letters, each one taking up the width of the doors. The letters were painted in red.

A 'W'.

An 'E'.

An 'L'.

'WELCOME'.

JB jumped down on to the pebbles to widen his vision. A gap, then two more beach huts. The second word came in to view: 'TO'.

He had to move down the beach to get the full picture until he was almost at the high tide mark, the sea straining to reach his trainers. A gap.

'S'

'H'

'I'

'T'

Another gap.

'T'

'O'

'W'

'N'

Normally he'd have laughed. Normally he'd have punched Scooby in the ribs and pointed and the two of them would have creased up and congratulated the artist who'd done it. Normally it would all be forgotten in an instant and he'd be on the next street already. The next time he passed the writing it would still be there but he wouldn't really look at it. Eventually, somebody would whitewash it out. There'd be a day or two and then another piece would spring up. Usually it was tagging. There were good taggers and bad taggers and it was easy to tell the difference. Mostly it was nothing, just some kid with a spray can making his mark.

This was different. He didn't feel the same about it. He felt a burning sensation, a feeling he hadn't experienced before, something pushing the rage to one side. He didn't know what it was. He let it sit there while he went to the storage shed and checked the broken wood. The hut would need a new door. He let it sit while he started the task of clearing up the spilled paint tins, starting with those nearest the threshold, reaching in and pulling them up from the puddle of yellow paint and then holding them at arm's length, carrying them out into the morning, spacing them out on the sea wall in the sun. He couldn't reach the tins at the back. He didn't want to step in the puddle of paint so he sat next to the paint tins on the wall and took a swig from his bottle of water.

That's when he noticed the four men coming through the sea grass. One was the big man from the float on carnival day. He was dressed in tight jeans and a maroon jumper and he was marching ahead, kicking up sand with each step. Then there was Swallow, quick-footed, lagging behind, apologetic. Behind the two of them, keeping some distance, were two men in dark uniforms. It took JB a moment before he realised what they were, it had been a while since he'd had the pleasure, but when he did his heart sank. They were police officers. They came straight at him, the square man all over the place, barely containing himself. JB knew that if the police hadn't been there the square man would have been on him. Swallow tried his best, but the square man was having none of it.

'He says he didn't do it,' said Swallow. 'Where I come from people are innocent until proven guilty and you don't have any proof.'

'Proof? Proof? He was seen. People saw him with their own eyes. People I trust.'

'Maybe they saw someone else.'

'I don't believe this. People like you, you're half the problem. You pull the wool over people's eyes. You run around making excuses for them so they carry on doing stuff like this. He's laughing at you, taking you for a ride.'

If he could have hit somebody he would have. JB watched as his face grew purple with rage, almost the same colour as the jumper he was wearing. The taller policeman was watching him carefully, too.

'How do you know it was him?' asked Swallow. 'They all wear the same clothes these days. I work with them and every time I see a lad with a hoodie I think it's one of my cases.'

'They should all be bloody made to wear orange suits so we know who they are.'

'He's not a terrorist!'

'I'm talking about boot camps. That's what we need. There's enough trouble in this town without you lot dragging some young criminal from the city down here. Especially this one. Two criminals in a tin-pot caravan together . . .'

'Okay, that's enough . . .'

The tall policeman stepped in.

'Oh, that's grand that is. Make me out to be the problem. I want him arrested and charged. It's about time you lot did something about kids like him. Put him on a recovery programme, set him up with a nice cushy number for the summer and this is how he repays the world . . . by laughing in its face.'

'If it was him we'll make sure he's charged accordingly. Now what

I'd like you to do is go home.'

'Bloody hell, even you lot are falling for it. The country's going to the dogs and you're the reason. They're everywhere. They're destroying everything this country stands for. They're parasites, feeding off those of us who give a damn. I built these bloody things. I built them for the good of the town. Stick him in borstal somewhere. Teach him some respect.'

His uncle appeared at the edge of the sea grass, a tiny figure with the marshes behind him. The dog was at his side, barking at the commotion. When the tall man saw him he pointed a finger and shouted.

'I knew he had something to do with you. I knew it when I saw him on carnival day. He's got that look about him.'

Despite the policemen flanking him on each side he carried on with the verbal assault.

'You shouldn't be here. Not after what you did. Nobody wants you here. Instead you start multiplying again, shoving another one of your stinking family on us. A hundred years ago they'd have lynched you for what you did. If I had my way they'd do it tomorrow . . .'

'Okay, sir, that's it.'

The two policemen grabbed the tall man by the arms and escorted him through the grass towards the caravan park. He carried on shouting with each step.

'If you don't calm down I'll be forced to arrest you.'

JB watched the theatre in front of him. Each time he tried to speak Swallow stopped him. It was like the courtroom with everybody having their say and him saying nothing. It was like he wasn't there at all. It was like they weren't talking about him but about someone else. He was powerless and irrelevant, but he would face the consequences of it all.

The big man was still shouting.

'Arrest me? You want to be arresting them, both of 'em. A yob and a murderer in the same caravan and you threaten me with arrest. That says it all.'

JB broke past Swallow and ran at the tall man, anger coursing through him, wanting to strike out, but when he got to the sea grass his legs wouldn't manage it and he stumbled forward. He wound up in a heap, the sea grass around his ears. His uncle came over and held out an arm, pulled him up with hands hard like leather and as coarse as sandpaper.

They stood and watched the men retreat till the splash of maroon was out of sight.

JB asked, 'What was that all about? All those things he said.'

'Don't listen to him. He's all hot air. He always has been.'

'You paint his huts?'

'They're not his. Just because he built the things. They're nothing to do with him any more, none except number seventy-seven. We don't do that one. When you get to it, miss it out.'

19

He waited for her on the sea wall, watching the sea and thinking about how it changed colour from one day to the next. The estate had never changed, had never looked like changing, but the sea was never the same twice. It was early evening. He had one hour before he had to be back at the caravan and as long as she came, as long as he had his time in her company, an hour would be enough.

But she didn't come. Instead he got a text message. She wasn't coming. She'd see him tomorrow. She'd explain then. She was sorry. He tried to fight against the ideas coming into his head, the idea that said her father was to blame, the idea that another thing in his life was being taken away.

He thought about returning to the caravan, decided against another night of sitting around waiting for another morning. He got up and started for the monument instead, to see if Moey's lot were there, to see what they knew about the graffiti.

Nobody was at the monument. It was quiet and peaceful there, the bronze boat still fighting the raging sea on top, the names still imprinted on the plaque. He walked on towards the harbour, a little nervous, keeping his head down, looking for signs of trouble. He passed a pub and looked in through the window to see a row of men at the bar, pints of beer resting in front of them, one of them telling a story, the others laughing along with it.

Further up the High Street was the supermarket. They were under the alcove there, sitting on the metal barrier that kept the trolleys in, the same gang as before. Lisette saw him first and ran up the road to meet him. She had a bottle in her hand.

'JB,' she screamed.

She stuffed an arm inside his and tottered back with him, unsteady on her feet. The clock outside the jewellers said it was quarter past six.

'We've been drinking all day,' she said. 'But I can't get drunk.'

The others turned their heads. The fat lad jumped down off the barrier. He lifted his hand to carry out the shake and JB responded, but he could see Moey looking at him and he didn't make a show of it.

'Look how drunk she is,' shouted the fat lad. 'She's only had two.'

'Two! What planet are you on? I've had four.'

'You've never had four! We only had ten in the first place.'

'I've had four. Fat tosser.'

'Go sister!'

When he reached the group he took his place on the edge of it. They were all drinking except Moey, who was fiddling with one of the trolleys, trying to separate it from the rest of the stack.

'Just stick a quid in,' said the lad with the bruises. They'd grown in size but faded now, to the colour of cold tea, surrounding his eyes with shadow.

'You stick a quid in,' said Moey. He carried on pulling and twisting at the chain and the attachment, swearing under his breath. The others watched him, only half-interested. JB thought of Scooby. They were the same in some ways, always doing something, always one step beyond. Lisette turned to him, her face pale, her eyes distant.

'What you been doing today? We've been drinking.'

Moey looked up.

JB said, 'Same old.'

'Painting those huts?' Moey asked.

'Yeah,' said JB.

Moey looked him in the eyes for a second or more, then went back to the trolley.

'I'm sick of this,' he said. 'You lot grab that one and we'll grab this one. We'll just pull 'em apart.'

The orders were carried out, Moey and bruise boy at one end, the fat lad and the little lad at the other. JB kept his distance, watched as they yanked the two trolleys apart, the chain holding its own. Then Moey swung a kick at it from underneath. The chain was taut and the kick made the difference. The trolleys separated and the fat lad fell backwards, landing in a heap by the supermarket doors.

Laughter erupted from the group. JB laughed too.

They wheeled the trolley down the high street, pushing it ahead of them at first and letting it free-wheel along the pavement, sometimes hitting shop windows and door frames, sometimes hitting lamp posts. Three times it ended up clattering into the gutter and three times they picked it up again. JB walked at the back of the group with the fat lad and Lisette. She stumbled along between the pair of them, her heels clicking on the concrete, the bottle in her hand no more than a fashion accessory now. It was obvious she was finished with drinking. When they reached the beach she flopped down and collapsed against a breaker. JB perched himself up on it, keeping a distance, watching Moey, trying to look nonchalant.

There was an old slipway at the beach and the trolley was perched on top of it now, a perverted toboggan. The little lad gave the trolley a shove. It set off down the slipway, careering left, finding a straight course, veering again. Each change in direction was greeted by cheers from the gang. When it hit the sand and pebbles of the beach it tipped forward and cart-wheeled over, landing on its side, its little wheels still turning. The little lad ran after it, pulled it back upright and then started the process of bringing it back. Moey laughed.

'Who's up for it then?'

'No way,' said the fat lad. 'Did you see how it flipped?'

'It wouldn't with you in it,' said Moey.

The group cackled.

'He wouldn't fit in the first place,' said the little lad.

More cackles, the sound carrying down the beach on the wind, causing a seagull to take to the air and move two breakers away from them, where it perched and watched, distrusting.

The lad with the bruises climbed into the trolley. Moey and the little lad waited until he was sat in it and then they pushed. The trolley took off at speed, stayed upright, stayed straight, hit the beach at pace and then flipped. The lad with the bruises dived head first from the cockpit, his arms flailing. He landed on his side and rolled to a stop then jumped to his feet and bowed, his face taut with laughter. Claps and cheers erupted from the gang.

'Showoff!'

'Just call me stuntman from now on . . .'

'Bring it back then.'

'I can do better!'

And so it went on, the little lad, the lad with the bruises again, this time flipping out sideways on to the slipway, getting up holding his elbow.

'Shit!'

'Some stuntman!'

'I don't see you trying it . . .'

'I'm saving myself.'

'Yeah, saving yourself from looking like a twat!'

More laughter. JB watched it all from the breaker. Lisette was down by his feet, laid out on the sand, the curve of her back touching the breaker, eyes closed, not asleep, just somewhere else. The second girl came over and bent down to examine her.

'She's well out of it!'

'Serves her right . . .'

'She's only had two!'

'More than you've had . . .'

Moey climbed into the trolley.

'All of you push me. Gimme some speed!'

And they did, the fat lad, the little lad, the lad with the bruises. The trolley started down the slipway and Moey tried to stand up in it. He almost managed it but the trolley turned to the right and he over-balanced. The trolley spewed him out. He landed on the slipway and rolled to the bottom, the trolley rolling after him, rolling into him, the whole event drawn out for full dramatic effect, accompanied by a random selection of shouts and sounds. The gang clapped and laughed, all except Lisette, who was completely out of it now, lying against the breaker at JB's feet.

Moey left the trolley on its side at the bottom of the slipway and started back up the slope, one eye on Lisette and JB. The fat lad shouted out.

'Bring it back then . . .'

'If you want it go and fetch it,' said Moey.

Nobody fetched it. Instead Moey grabbed three of the empty bottles and set off back down the slipway to the breaker. He set them up on one of the wooden posts, came back and started to fire pebbles at them, taking aim and throwing with as much force as he could muster so that when the pebbles missed the bottles and hit the wood there was a loud crack of sound. The others joined in, JB too, each one taking their turn with a pebble.

The little lad hit first but it was a weak throw and it only succeeded in knocking the bottle off the post.

'Put it back,' said Moey. 'You've got to smash the things.'

When the little lad went down to pick up the bottle Moey and the lad with the bruises threw pebbles at him instead, aiming to miss, firing at his feet and at the wooden barrier for sound effects.

'Oi! Watch it! You're mental!'

Then they went back to throwing at the bottles until each one was smashed to pieces and the shards of glass were littered over the beach on either side of the breaker.

'Hey, watch this,' said the fat lad. He ran down the beach to the spot where the bottles had been and took something out of his pocket. He dropped to his knees at the barrier. JB watched him. He watched him with a sick feeling rising in his stomach. The fat lad had a spray can. When he'd finished he stood back and turned around, grinning from ear to ear. Behind him on the barrier in red-coloured paint were the words, 'BEWARE GLASS'.

He stood back and surveyed his handiwork for five seconds, milking his moment in the spotlight, milking it too long, until the moment was gone, until the gang had their backs to him and were all around Lisette up at the breaker, trying to get her to her feet. Her body was limp and the most she could mutter were feeble groans. JB knelt down at her side to see what he could do and that was when she threw up, purple-coloured liquid sick that ran into the pebbles and sprayed on to his trainers. Moey burst into laughter.

The other girl stepped in then, taking over where the lads were useless.

'It's not funny. Get her some water, someone. If she goes home in this state her dad'll kill her.'

'Yeah, get us some fags as well,' said Moey.

The little lad, the fat lad and the lad with the bruises trudged off up the beach while the other girl sat Lisette upright and wiped her face with a tissue. JB jumped up on to the breaker and Moey joined him there.

'How did you get on with that stuff?' asked Moey.

'Yeah, it was all right,' JB lied. He wondered if it showed, looked up at the lads as they scaled the steps at the sea wall and disappeared over the top.

'It's wicked, mate. Let me know when you want more.'

JB sensed his moment.

'Did you hear about that writing on the huts?'

Moey looked at him and grinned.

'Hilarious.'

'They're blaming me for it.'

Moey shrugged.

'So what?'

'Well, to you it'd just be a slap on the wrist but they could stick me away.'

'Shouldn't have done it then, should you?'

Moey smiled.

JB looked at him, thinking about where this was heading, trying to see through Moey but seeing nothing. They both turned their heads to Lisette and the other girl instead.

'Stupid cow,' said Moey. 'She knows she can't handle her drink but every time she drinks the most. You're welcome to her.'

'Me?'

JB felt his cheeks reddening despite himself.

'In your dreams,' said Moey. 'She's my bitch.'

'Don't call her that,' said the other girl.

'Why not?'

'Because . . .'

'Because what?'

JB left them to it, started up the beach to the sea wall, letting the sound of his feet on the pebbles hide all other sounds.

The others came back. They had chocolate and crisps and water. The fat lad opened his jacket. Underneath were six bottles of beer. They shared them out. The fat lad offered the last one to JB but JB shook his head.

'I'm off back,' he said.

'Already?'

'He's got to get in or he'll turn into a pumpkin,' laughed Moey.

The others laughed too. It was automatic. Moey said something and laughed, everybody else laughed with him. Like a recording.

He sent Sal a text when he got in and waited but no text came back. He sat with his thumb on the buttons, wanting to send another and another until she replied, typing-deleting, typing-deleting. Waiting.

His uncle came back from the allotment and cooked up some burgers and chips. JB ate his on the stone steps outside the caravan, tossing chips to the dog when he felt like it. When it turned cold he went in and made up his bed, listened to the faint sound of his uncle's radio beyond the curtain. His uncle was listening to the shipping forecast and JB listened too, not really hearing it, just letting it exist on the edge of his being, drifting off to sleep with it there, using it for company, enjoying the comfort of it.

20

In the morning he painted half a hut and then gave up. His head was full. He walked to her house instead, determined to see her, but he stopped when he got to the gate. He couldn't do it. What if her father was in? What if he saw him standing there at the end of his garden path? He hung around until a neighbour came out and started staring and then he started back.

He was full of nervous energy so he ran along the footpath, reaching the horses in the meadow. The grey horse was close to the fence, the black horse way over in the shade of the trees, hardly visible. He didn't stop. Instead he skipped down the steps three at a time to the sea wall and ran back to the site. He vaulted over the gate and raced across the field to the caravan, thinking about getting something to eat, thinking about catching up with the painting, thinking about anything but Sal. A man was standing by the door. He was carrying a briefcase.

'Is this number 16?'

'Who wants to know?' asked JB.

The man's eyes narrowed.

'Tristan Bellows,' he said. 'I'm looking for Jason Bridge, who is not where he is meant to be at the time he's meant to be there.'

'That's me,' said JB. 'What's the problem? Where's Baz?'

'You're Jason Bridge?'

JB nodded.

'If you mean Barry Swallow, he's been withdrawn from your case.'

'Why?'

'That's not for me to say.'

'It's because of the graffiti, right? I told them I had nothing to do with it.'

'This would be the vandalism of the beach huts?'

'Vandalism? Yeah. Yeah, I suppose so.'

'I think that might have had something to do with it. It doesn't exactly impress the local community when things like that appear.'

'So it doesn't matter that I had nothing to do with it? When do I get to see Baz?'

'He's been reassigned.'

JB opened up the caravan. The musty darkness tried to escape but the daylight kept it in check. He stepped into it while Bellows hesitated at the door. He hadn't bothered to make up his bed. He stretched over the rumpled covers and switched on the lamp but it made next to no difference. Only the strip light made a difference inside and it ate up too much of the meter to use in the daytime. JB opened the curtains as far as they'd go and tied them back with the loose strings that were hanging there. Expertly, feeling the new man standing in the doorway watching him, he set about making the bed into a sofa too. It took him thirty seconds, plus another thirty to put the table back up. Bellows edged inside and sat down. He put his briefcase on the table and flicked it open, started to leaf through a pile of papers.

JB filled the kettle and put it on the stove. He lit the gas burner and waited for the kettle to boil. For a time the only sound was the hiss of the gas and the slow steaming of the kettle. JB got two mugs down from the shelf above the window and chucked a tea-bag in each one.

'Er, not for me thanks,' said Bellows.

'You sure?' asked JB. 'Baz always has one.'

'I try not to drink hot drinks,' Bellows said, still fussing with the papers, flicking them over in his fingers.

'Not even in winter?'

'No, never,' said Bellows.

'Why not?' asked JB. 'They warm you up, they freshen you up . . .'

'I just don't drink hot drinks,' said Bellows. He took the pile of papers from the briefcase and knocked them together three times while he waited for JB to finish. JB poured the water from the kettle into one of the mugs and reached under the sink for the milk. He came up with a carton of long-life stuff.

'I don't like it, but it's all we've got . . .'

'Excuse me, but we really need to discuss the situation,' said Bellows. He shifted in his seat.

'Sure,' said JB. 'Go ahead.'

'Well,' said Bellows. 'I'll start with today. Your agreement clearly states that between the hours of nine in the morning and four in the afternoon you are to be located at the beach huts opposite this site, unless the weather is poor in which case you are to be here at the caravan or on site assisting others in site upkeep. When I arrived at eleven-thirty this morning you were neither at the beach huts or on site. At twelve-fifteen you arrive back here.'

'I was on lunch break.'

'Your agreement clearly states that all lunch breaks are to be held at the beach huts or indeed here at this very table. It also states that you take this break between the times of 1 and 2 p.m.'

'That's just what it says on the paper,' said JB.

'It doesn't "just" say anything. It clearly states that you are to be in a specific place at a specific time.'

'Well, it isn't the Bible, is it?'

Bellows placed the palms of his hand over the order.

'You're mistaken, Jason. The paper is the only thing keeping you out of a young offenders' centre. I will have to report this.'

'Baz didn't worry about things like that. He came to have a chat and a cup of tea. Baz was all right.'

'I shall have to report that as well. I know why you're here, Jason. I've read all of the files. Throwing snowballs at the elderly, smashing up abandoned cars, verbal assault, disturbing the peace, damaging and destroying property. This is not a holiday. You'd do well to remember that.'

'Half of them were lies or nothing to do with me.'

'Even half makes grim reading. I'm not like Barry Swallow. I think this ASBO is the best thing that could have happened to you. And if you break it, then a detention training order and two years in a detention centre will teach you a lesson you'll never forget. You're very lucky your mother won them over and convinced them you could do this. If you were still up there I'd give you a week at most before you broke it.'

'You'd break it too if they banned you from where you live.'

'But they won't ban me from where I live, because I respect where I live and I respect who I live by. That's the difference, Jason. That's what you need to learn.'

'I didn't do anything different to loads of lads . . .'

Bellows nodded his head.

'Yes. I'm inclined to agree with you there. But don't worry about that. You're the first of many, I'm sure.'

Silence. Bellows eyeing the caravan, making notes with a silver ballpoint, JB sipping tea and watching him, bewildered.

'I have to say, I thought your uncle would be around.'

'He'll be at the allotment.'

'Hmmm.'

Half a cold cup of tea in his palms, forms filled, boxes ticked, JB watched Bellows plod awkwardly across the field to his car. A dog barked and Bellows swivelled comically. When he got to his car he reached inside, took a cloth and wiped the bottom of his feet with it before climbing in. Very carefully, he manoeuvered his car forwards and backwards until he was in a position to drive away. JB watched Bellows' car disappear up the beach road, wishing he could be in some place where nobody could find him.

21

Hut fifty-seven. Blue. JB busy. Sal sitting on the wall with her bag full of books, sitting on her hands, kicking her legs out, acting like the days before hadn't happened.

'My mum is trying to move here. It's some new scheme,' said JB.

'There's the Watts Estate.'

'The estate by the railway?'

'Yeah . . . but I didn't mean it like that . . .'

'At least it's not the city.'

'I thought you loved it there.'

'I do, but there's my sister. It'd be great for her, just getting fresh air and stuff. And there's shops there. They're all shut on our estate, apart from the bookies and the kebab place. But that won't stay open much longer. Too much trouble.'

'That happens here too. It's funny. I'm trying to get away and your mum wants to come here.'

'You're mad leaving.'

'You're mad staying,' she laughed.

'Right. Like I have a choice.'

'Sorry. I didn't mean it like that . . .'

'Shouldn't you be reading or something . . .'

'Why? Trying to get rid of me?'

'Yeah. I'd much rather be all alone with my brushes . . .'

He laughed. She laughed. He threatened her with the paint brush and she recoiled.

'Don't you dare.'

The day ticked on regardless but at least she was here with him.

She was silent for long spells. He threw glances at her between brush-strokes, watched her eyes dance across the pages on her lap. Later, when he stopped to drink a can of Coke, a new expression on her face.

'My dad says you should ask your uncle about what happened. Then you'd know why he treated you the way he did.'

'What's my uncle got to do with it?'

'I'm just saying . . .'

'You can tell your dad I've got better things to be doing than getting up in the night to write messages to ships . . .'

'I did . . .'

'And . . . ?'

'It doesn't matter.'

'Exactly.'

'He says you were seen and that's the end of it. And he didn't like it that I'd spoken to you.'

He shook his head and started away from her, belched silently from the drink.

'Just because he lives up here. Just because he keeps himself to himself.'

'I'm just telling you . . .'

'Don't bother. You're as bad as they are.'

'Jay!'

'Not looking . . .'

'Jay!'

'Not listening . . .'

'Jay! They say he killed two people.'

'Who?'

'Your uncle.'

'Who says?

'My dad. Others. Everybody.'

'How?'

'I don't know. On a boat. A fishing boat. Something like that.'

'That's stupid.'

'It's what they say . . .'

'And you believe them?'

'Jay, my dad says that's what happened. Why would he lie about something like that?'

'He's lying about me and all this . . .'

'He's not lying. He believes you did it. That's different.'

'Not for me it isn't. He doesn't know me. He doesn't even want you talking to me. You don't know me. What are you here for?'

'You won't let me talk to you. I'm only trying to help.'

'Yeah? Well, I don't need it.'

'Thanks, Jay,' she said. 'Thanks a lot.'

'What happened to you these last few days?' he asked.

She opened her mouth to speak, was about to say something, and then she walked away instead, between the huts, over the sea grass, leaving him there on the beach, the whole thing happening suddenly, like a sea storm blowing through, leaving him there on the beach like something washed up by the tide.

22

For a long time, he sat by the huts and let his mind float over every-thing. The evening light was severe, cutting its way through the land-scape, casting a blinding white sheen on the water, the caravans, the beach huts, his domain. The shadows stretched away from the sun, creating distorted forms that seemed to shrink away in terror. The marshes stretched away too, somehow lengthened by the light. The earth clinging to the light, as if unwilling to lose it, the shadows stretching and stretching until it seemed to him that they'd break. Still he sat there. He had questions to ask his uncle. He had things he needed to tell Sal too, but they were all stacked up behind a wall and he couldn't break the wall down. The light lost its edge, turned pink and softened the surroundings. The ocean settled into its own gentle rhythm, a regular accompaniment of sound, each settling wave mimicking the one before it.

It was funny how quickly one set of things took over from another. He hadn't thought about the estate all day. Instead his head had been full of the graffiti, Sal's father, her coming to see him. He thought about the estate now though, but not in the way he expected. For the first time he missed the flight of stairs that led to his flat, the scratched red door, the smell of his mother's air fresheners, the sofa where he'd flopped so often, his sister running up to him, grabbing his leg, trying to get him to play games, his room, his TV, his bed.

He got up and started through the sea grass to the caravan park. There was a single light on in the caravan, the light at his uncle's end. A sudden rush of determination came over him. He would look his uncle in the eye and ask him the question right out and he'd know in that moment if he was lying or telling the truth. But when he opened the door his uncle wasn't there, and instead of talk he had to make himself beans on toast and sit with the TV on. The news came on and he watched it absently until they started talking about how a foot-baller had to wear a tag for drink-driving and how it stuck out from inside his sock when he was playing. He wondered how the tag might feel to wear, if it would itch like a plaster when you broke a bone. Then they started talking about how some team was about to buy a player for thirty million quid instead. Afterwards there was a weather fore-cast. A smiling man came on and talked about the weather they'd been having, then his face changed and he started to talk about a storm coming in, a big one. He advised people to stay indoors.

Later JB went to the door to find the dog sat beside it. The evening was charged with electricity. He could feel the storm. The air was heavy as if a great weight were pressing down upon it. There was an eerie silence beyond the caravan park, a feeling of something yet to begin. In the pastel light, JB noticed the flood barriers had been erected at the entrance, the wooden slats in place between the concrete posts. He listened for birds but he could not hear a single one calling. He saw a curtain flapping in the window of one of the cara-vans. An arm reached up and slammed the window shut. Soon after, the woman with the cats came out on to the steps and called 'Ginger' three times until the little ginger kitten darted out from behind the dustbins and leapt into the caravan. The dog watched it go and JB watched the dog, one hand on its neck fur just in case. The woman gave JB a little wave and then disappeared in after the cat. He heard the bolt shoot across and lock in place. Way over to his left a black block of cloud was forming and while he stood there watching he saw the first leading edges of the storm arrive. Gently, hardly visible had he not been looking directly at it, the washing line started to quiver in the breeze. A moment later and he felt the heat drain from the evening and the hairs on his arms stand upward. Goose pimples appeared on his skin. A tree branch trembled as if the tree itself were aware of the battering it was soon to take and wanted to uproot and escape, but the tree was fixed to the caravan park much like he was fixed and the tree would have to bear up to it like he was about to bear up to it. He thought about his uncle. He wondered where he was. He had a feeling something big was on its way, something he didn't truly understand.

He stepped back inside the caravan, turned up the TV and tried to forget about it, but he couldn't, not here. Every now and then he went over to the window and peered out from behind the curtains. The sky darkened. The washing line grew steadily busier, flapping back and forth, the metal pole rocking gently in the baked summer earth.

He was sat on the bed when the door swung open and his uncle came in. A newspaper flapped around until the door was closed again.

'Looks like we're in for one tonight . . .'

JB shrugged.

' . . . you wait and see. Sitting out one of these in a thing like this . . . feels like you're on a boat on the ocean . . .'

'Some chance of that,' said JB.

'One of those days?' asked his uncle.

'Every day is one of those days,' said JB.

The storm came in hard and fast, like a rage was being spent on the coastline. The caravan rocked on its moorings. JB watched from his bed, peered through the window as the tree branches bent back at impossible angles and stray rubbish flew across the field, got caught up in the leaves and then flew onward across the marshes. The window shook in its frame, and the wind raced under the caravan and around it, squealing and screaming like a thousand demons. When darkness descended the storm remained. JB lay in his bed listening to it happening around him. He was trapped and powerless as the dark energy launched itself on the world.

23

Cash in the giro
Hold on or let go
Forget your fate
On this estate

Find your own crew
Break out or break through
Forget your fate
On this estate

Go with the way you feel
Do what makes it real
Check out the fertility rate
On this estate

They said it was a community centre but mostly it was a crèche and nursery for the young mothers on the Jubilee Estate. For a little while it had been a youth club but the funding had dried up and there were no volunteers to do it for nothing. Besides, when it had been a youth club there had been too much trouble; gang fights, vandalism, criminal damage, abuse of the youth workers. Nobody really believed in it any more, and so it had stood empty after dark.

Except for this night. The early evening storm had moved away and after it had gone the people had appeared and disappeared inside the community centre doors so that this night it was full to bursting.

The strip lights were on and the harsh light flooded from the windows on to the grassy wasteland of the kiddies' playground. Chairs had been set out in rows facing one end, facing a single row of chairs that were turned towards them. The single row of chairs was outnumbered by ten to one and each chair that was in the majority was occupied by a tenant of the estate. Hot air filled the room and the windows were steamed over, tiny droplets of condensation forming on the glass, the biggest droplets no longer able to cling to the surface, already running down to the sill, leaving thin trails and streaks. Puddles were forming on the sill itself and a little boy was playing with one of them, dipping his finger in and running it along the sill to create a pattern. His mother tugged at his coat sleeve and tried to get him to sit on her knee but the boy was intent only on the window and the patterns and he pulled his arm away. The noise coming from the room was a jumble of voices, as though someone had caught a hundred sets of vocal cords in a box, shaken them around and then taken the lid off, and each voice was anxious and angry and ready.

Stuck on various walls and doors was the same poster. It showed the picture of a sixteen-year-old boy. He was staring at the camera, his eyes vacant and listless. The picture was of JB. Above the picture was one word, 'ASBO' and underneath it a message.

'JASON BRIDGE is banned from the following locations under an Anti-Social Behaviour Order:

The area immediately outside the shops and properties on Jubilee Road.

The area that lies within the boundaries of King George Court, King Charles Road and Queen Mary's Road.

If you see this boy in these areas he is in breach of the Anti-Social Behaviour Order taken out against him and is committing a criminal act. Report such instances to the police.'

A door opened at the front of the room and a line of people stepped from it into the light. A large woman came first. She was dressed in a suit but the suit was worn at the edges, as if perhaps it was the only one she owned. She was carrying a brown leather wallet full of papers and the wallet had seen better days, too. The woman was trying to smile and look assured but there were tell-tale signs behind her glasses that she was sitting on a time bomb that one day she knew would explode. Behind her came two policemen. They were dressed in uniform and supporting a senior officer who was dressed immaculately in his own uniform. His silver hair shone under the strip lights and his white teeth shone too when he smiled. He sat down next to the woman with the leather wallet. The line was completed by three party representatives, each presented in the familiar colours: red, blue, yellow.

Each of these people took a seat at the front of the hall and stared out over the sea of faces opposite. Only the senior police officer stared back at the group with any grace and conviction. He smiled at the small boy stood by the window and the small boy buried his head in his chest. A busy-looking man in brown cords and a leather jacket stepped out of the crowd and over to the single microphone. He tapped the microphone twice and then coughed before finally getting to grips with it and calling out for quiet. Having gained the attention of the audience, he started to speak.

'Ladies and gentlemen, residents of the Jubilee Estate, can I have your attention please. Thank you . . . thank you . . .'

The lid fell on the box of vocal cords. Somewhere towards the back a baby girl mewed softly while her young mother struggled to cope, but this was the only sound to breach the silence. The busy man held his breath for a moment and then began again.

'Thanks for coming down . . . thanks for attending . . . this annual meeting . . . a few more here than in previous years . . .'

The busy man laughed quietly to himself but the atmosphere failed to soften. Instead he started to look increasingly awkward.

'Let me quickly introduce you to who we have here tonight and then we can begin . . .'

The sea of faces fell on the people at the front and the people at the front stared out over their heads, all except the police officer who was now trying to avoid making eye contact with a single living soul.

An hour later the meeting was in full flow.

It had started quietly with the speakers in control and the audience listening, but now things were open to the floor and the lid had come off the box again. The busy man was struggling to cope with it all and the voices sprouted from the mass like rogue weeds.

'You say you're getting on top of the crime on the estate but I've had my car vandalised three times in the last two months . . .'

'They roam around like animals and don't have respect for anyone or anything . . .'

'One question at a time please!'

'All you seem to want to do is tell us about a load of fancy numbers. We don't give a damn about your numbers. We want to see someone on the street making arrests . . .'

'I've already said . . . the Anti-Social Behaviour legislation has been put in place to tackle those individuals who fail to behave in a socially acceptable way and as you are aware that is already becoming effective on this estate . . .'

'Effective! Come and take a look at my garden fence . . .'

The man with the red tie: 'We're adopting a very strict policy on all those individuals. They will be named in the community. You might have seen some of the posters we've had printed. The newspapers are supporting us one hundred per cent. We're able to use these orders to keep the worst cases off our streets. There are already several curfews in place, keeping individuals in their homes between 7 p.m. and 7 a.m. every day. If they break those curfews they're in danger of arrest and further prosecution. It's proving very successful. One particular case has resulted in the offender being removed from the estate altogether.'

Laughter. Jeers. Ignored.

'We're taking a hard line on all instances of anti-social behaviour. We believe it's the only way to make a difference. And yes, we are acting like parents. If parents cannot control their children then it is up to us to take action, against the children and against the parents.'

Shouting and swearing. Heat and sweat building.

Another hour. Question time. JB's mother stood up in the hall. She meant to ask a question, but something took over her at the last second. Perhaps it was the smile on the large woman's face. Perhaps it was the high-and-mighty attitude of the residents. Once she stood up and started, she couldn't stop.

'Mrs Abigail Bridge. Resident. Ashamed to be after tonight. My son is the one who has his face slapped all over the estate on your wanted poster. I can't believe what I've been hearing. Listen to the lot of you, forgetting when you were kids. I remember some of you from back then. You were the same. You, Sally Weatherall. I remember you getting drunk around the back of the launderette and throwing up on a car bonnet. John Figgins. How many times were you in trouble for vandalism?'

'I never nicked a car . . .'

'No, but you smashed one in. And you put a brick through the Mace window. Put the shopkeeper in hospital as well . . .'

'Your bloody husband was hardly a stranger to the law!'

'Shut up, you cow!'

'Mrs Bridge! Mrs Bridge!'

But she was away now and nothing was going to stop her. This had been building for a long, long time, all through the stuff with Jay, all through the stuff that came before. She pointed a finger at the MP.

'And you lot! You're the worst. You come down here from your posh houses up on Fellows Road or somewhere, you spout off about how the kids down here need a severe lesson, you come up with some rubbish about cutting crime by chucking a load of meaningless numbers at us and then you think you can swan off back home and we'll all rush down to the polling station on election day and sign a little box with your name against it. Then we won't see hide nor hair of any of you down here for another four years or however long it is they stick people like you on those comfy seats up there in Parliament. I've seen you sleeping on TV. I've seen you on the news, sitting there laughing with each other when you're supposed to be debating our kids' futures. Now you think it's okay to name and shame my child for the things he's done wrong. You think it's going to make him responsible. Maybe you should name and shame the people who've sent me letters since your posters went up and your newsletters were shoved through our doors. Letters telling me if they see my son around here again they'll kill him. Letters telling me that I have no right to have

children. Letters telling me to turn to God to be forgiven for my sins
as a mother!'

The three men at the front tried to speak, almost started, never
made it.

'Maybe you should name and shame the real criminals, the drug
pushers who are selling the stuff to our kids in the first place. Did you
know there have been two armed robberies around here in the last
month? Not to mention the burglaries. There's your real criminals.
There's who you should be after. But no. Instead you pick out some
sixteen-year-old lad who hasn't got the sense to see what it's all about
yet because his dad buggered off and his mother has had it hard
trying to keep in a job and raise him properly. You chuck him out of
school, splash his picture all over the place and tell him what an
animal he is, make it illegal for him to walk the streets he grew up on
and then tell me that if I don't pack him off somewhere else you'll
arrest him next time he steps out of our front door. Grown men with
guns get better treatment.

'I'll tell you now if they take me on that moving scheme you won't
see me for dust. I'm not ashamed to say it. This estate was never
perfect but it was never like this, never so full of people with everything to lose and nothing to gain from helping each other. You all
make me sick. You know why I sent him away? Not for the reasons you
think. I did it to save him from you lot.'

She sank backwards on her legs as if the force of the moment had
taken the last remaining energy from her body. A few people shouted
encouragement and somebody clapped, but most just sat and waited
to see what was going to happen next. Somewhere at the side of the
room a photographer was leaning in, his camera set, trying to get a
shot of her. There was a bright flash of light.

The representative with the red tie stood up and pulled the microphone towards him.

'Perhaps I can say a few things now. This is not about criminalising your son. It is about protecting others from anti-social behaviour and . . .'

A voice cut in.

'How about giving the kids something to do . . .'

Another, louder, mocking.

'That's been tried . . . they don't respect it and they don't appreciate it!'

'They're kids!'

Aggressive.

'They're bloody old enough to have sex though, and to drink, and smoke that stuff that's infesting the whole of society . . .'

Pleading.

'Ladies and gentlemen! Can we have *one* meeting please?'

She got up, pushed through the crowd behind her and out of the door. She was fine with it all until she was outside, until she looked up at the hundreds of square lights in the tower block and the group of lads and lasses grouped together at the kiddies' playground, huddled together like lost souls, their hoodies up so they could have been anybody, could have been her son, and that caused the tears to come flooding out of her, all the tears she'd saved in the weeks that had passed since they'd forced her to send her son away to keep him out of prison.

24

JB woke to an empty sky. He peeked at it from behind the curtain, a perfect blue sky that stretched away forever. He could hear the birds singing, crying out their early morning chorus. The marshes were alive with dancing insects and brightly coloured flowers. It was easy to think the storm had never happened and if he'd kept his eyes on the sky and the marshes he might have managed it, but his eyes dropped to the caravan site and the true story reared up beyond the window. The roof to the toilet block was gone. The storm had stripped the tarpaulin and the tiles away so that now there was just the empty shell. One of the caravans had slipped from its foundations, or the foundations had collapsed somehow, so that it was tilted at an angle. Three or four people were already gathered around it. They had ropes and they were pointing and talking. One of the men was his uncle.

The rest of the caravans seemed okay. Some had lost their TV aerials. Loose wires trailed from the rooftops but the aerials were nowhere to be seen. The washing line had survived but the pole was bent right over and the concrete base had uprooted itself from the earth like old tree roots were sometimes uprooted. The tree that had trembled the night before was still there but it didn't look the same. Some of its branches had snapped and were dangling pathetically. It had lost leaves and looked a bare and pale shadow of what it had been the day he'd sat under it and thought about Sal. The moment she dropped into his head the protective feeling came over him again. He tried to let it settle but it would not. He wondered what else the storm had done. He tried the TV but it wasn't working so he turned on the radio instead. It crackled into life and told its stories. Somewhere amongst all of the carnage, people had died. It was on the radio as he swigged his tea and made ready to go and see how the huts had fared. A driver had been crushed by a fallen tree. Someone else had been hit by falling debris. JB only caught a bit of it but somewhere they were carrying out a sea search-and-rescue for a missing person. He wanted Sal to be sat here in the caravan with him so he could look at her and know she was okay. He thought about her during the time it took him to wash and dress. He was still thinking about her when he closed the caravan door behind him and stepped down into the grass to check out the huts. The ground underneath the sea grass was saturated with water and each step he made produced a squelching sound. By the time he got through it his jeans were soaked to his knees, but there was a light summer breeze and the sun was warm and he knew he would dry out soon enough.

He was about to slip between the huts when the air around him started to shake. A thunderous sound came from above and a moment later a helicopter rushed overhead, its yellow paintwork pristine against the blue sky, its rotor blades spinning in black circles. It was low to the ground, heading along the coast. By the time he moved from between the huts to the sea wall it was already out over the water, so low that the seawater beneath it rippled outwards. He watched it head off towards Haycliffe, expecting it to disappear over the horizon but it didn't. Because it was upwind he could still hear its rotor blades. He heard the sound alter as the helicopter swung across to the right and then began a sweep back up the channel. Closer and closer it came until it was over him again and then, just as quickly as it had come, the sound diminished to almost nothing, carried down the coast on the breeze.

He was standing on the sea wall surveying the huts when the helicopter made its third pass. He knew then what was going on. They were searching his section of coastline. He looked out to sea. They were looking for somebody. In his mind he caught a snapshot of a body on the beach, a limp, lifeless shape, the crabs already at the flesh, the eyes staring upwards, wide open but seeing nothing. In an instant his own eyes scanned the section of beach in front of him, but there was nothing to see, just the shallow waves gently lapping at the shore, the odd trailing strip of seaweed.

Hut sixty-eight. (Yellow.) The fat lad appeared on the sea wall. JB was surprised to see him on his own. It usually didn't happen like that. He was used to seeing them together, like a pack of dogs or something. They were like that, biting and snapping, hunting together. On his own the fat lad looked lost and laughable.

'All right JB?' he shouted.

JB nodded.

'Moey sent me to tell you. They're all at the harbour waiting to see . . .'

'To see what?'

'To see who they're going to bring in . . .'

They both ducked down as the helicopter made another sweep of the water.

'It's one of the lifeboat men, I think. That's why Moey sent me. He said you'd want to know that.'

JB's heart was close to bursting in his chest, the sea wall a long strip of white behind him and a long strip of white in front of him. It didn't matter how fast his legs worked, he didn't feel like he was getting anywhere. But he knew where he had to be. He had to be at Sal's side, because if it was Sal's father, if it was him, then nothing else mattered except finding her and being there for her. The beach was littered with debris from the storm. It was spread out from the surf line to the flood barriers and it was impossible to tell where the high tide mark was. The natural order of things had been turned on its head. Driftwood had been discarded high up on the wall in one place. In another, an empty wheelie bin had been transferred down the beach almost as far as the water. It lay on its side in the small pebbles, looking like a beached whale.

He found her at the harbour. She was standing amongst the lobster pots, hiding from the scene that was playing out around her. She had a distant look on her face and for the first thirty seconds he was too scared to approach her. The harbour was busy with frantic people, a boat moving out towards the open water, moving out to join the search-and-rescue operation, the helicopter buzzing overhead.

'Sal,' he said.

She turned towards him and he knew. In truth he'd known since the moment the fat lad had told him, but now her stare affirmed everything. Now he was with her, though, he didn't know what to do. He stood, waiting for her to say something instead. She was looking at him but her eyes were really seeing something else and then she slumped backward on to the pots. Instinctively he went to move towards her but she shied away from him.

'Sal,' he said again.

But he might as well have not been there. He sat on the pots at her side and watched her from out of the corner of his eye. The rest of his vision was filled with the harbour and the water, some of the men in bright yellow or orange life-jackets, others in the thick jumpers that signalled they were fishermen, each one busy or trying to be busy, trying to do something when really there was nothing to be done except hope. Another boat entered the harbour and the men on board shouted from it towards the shore. After that, everything fell into slow motion. The man on the bow lifted something in front of him. It was sodden and heavy and when the man held it up huge droplets of water dripped from it towards the floor. It looked black at first but as the water was expelled from it a new colour emerged, a dark maroon colour. JB knew he'd seen the colour before. It was the final confirmation. He turned to look at Sal. She was staring at the jumper, lost for a moment, and then she burst into tears. This time, when JB reached out for her, she collapsed into him weakly. He held her as she sobbed, one arm folded around her shoulders, the other around her waist, and he watched as the boat reached its moorings and the men tied the ropes in place, watched the man with the jumper climb the metal ladder and show it to another man on the harbour wall. The second man nodded and then pointed towards JB and Sal. The man with the jumper made a ridiculous attempt to hide it but was too late.

JB pulled Sal closer.

'That doesn't mean anything,' he said, but his voice was weak and feeble and carried no conviction at all. As soon as he opened his mouth he wished he'd said nothing.

It was okay to say the discovery of the jumper could mean all sorts of things but he knew the truth of it. It was written on the faces of the fishermen and the rescue teams. It was written in the muffled sobs coming from Sal and it was punctuated by the brilliant yellow sheen of the helicopter as it swung around in the sky above them. They'd go on looking because it was their duty to look, but the men knew the water temperatures and the men knew the tides and just because nobody wanted to be the first to say, that didn't mean there was any more of a chance for Sal's father. They knew a man couldn't ask the sea for a chance, he could only take one with it and hope his luck held out.

JB found himself thinking about his uncle. It would have happened much like this, with everybody pulling together, everybody sharing the weight of the tragedy. Except that somewhere along the way the well of sympathy had dried out, so that slowly, over time, the weight of the tragedy had been dropped on his uncle's shoulders, a weight too heavy to be one man's burden.

The gang appeared. They were on the other side of the harbour, hanging around near the fish stall. The fat lad had caught up with them again so that there were four of them. Moey was in the middle. The same challenging feeling came over JB and once again his thoughts turned towards his uncle. He had been a local once, a respected fisherman, a drinking buddy. He had been all of those things and yet the community had shunned him. JB was none of those things. He was already suspected of the beach hut graffiti. Now a wave of fear came over him. It was ridiculous and over-dramatic and it made no sense at all, but he felt it all the same. It was telling him to get away from the harbour as soon as possible, telling him to go, before somebody saw an opportunity to drain the well and blame him, but as he looked over at Moey and the rest of them, he felt as though the well was already drained.

He walked Sal back through the town. She didn't want to go and she resisted at first but she was dead on her feet and in the end he forced her. He thought that she'd collapse at any moment. They kept to the back streets so they wouldn't meet people who wanted to ask questions and then they climbed the hill to her house. She left him at the gate. He stopped and she simply continued walking so they became separated in one flowing movement. Before she reached the door her mother opened it and she was transferred into another set of arms.

JB headed back to the caravan, hopping over the flood barriers on to the beach. It wasn't long before the helicopter rushed over him again. A group of people were stood on the sea wall watching it. He wanted to tell them to stop, that it wasn't something to get excited about, but he didn't say anything.

He went back to the huts and worked, splashing the yellow paint on the wood in heavy globules, not caring if it spilled from the brush on to the sea wall. He hated that he was using yellow. It made him think of the helicopter, so that it was always in his mind, either buzzing overhead or there in the tin in front of him. When the hut was finished he went back to the caravan and crashed out on his bed. All the while there was the distant thunder of the helicopter to contend with, pulling him back from the edge of sleep every time it made a pass. It was long after dark when the helicopter disappeared for good and the sleep he'd been searching for finally came upon him.

He dreamed she was alone in the house when he came looking for her, but she wouldn't answer the door. He'd come all the way in the darkness and now he was here she wouldn't let him in. She was hiding behind the curtains, hiding from him, pretending not to notice him, but he knew she was hiding and every second he stood at the gate his insides twisted a little tighter. A man appeared from the shadows. He had big square shoulders. He was wearing a maroon jumper, carrying a torch. It was Sal's father. He shone the blinding light into JB's eyes.

He had something in his other hand and he was wielding it like a weapon.

'Get away from here!'

He swung the thing in his hand at JB and JB fell backwards on to the path. He had time to get his hands up in front of him and then Sal's father swung the thing again.

'Get up! Get up and take it like a man!'

Each time JB tried to get up Sal's father battered him back to the ground. It went on and on, attack after attack forcing JB into pathetic submission.

His uncle woke him. He was standing over the bed.

'Jay. Wake up. It's morning.'

The sun was streaming through the window, the air in the caravan stuffy. JB's throat was parched with it. The sky was blue beyond the glass, the opposite of a nightmare.

Hut sixty-nine. Hut seventy. The days passing in a blur of sunlight and colour, the details of the tragedy unfolding in fragments, a picture building, a sea storm, a search-and-rescue mission for a vessel that didn't exist, the dark unsettling fear growing inside of him that somehow he would be blamed, and all the time Sal was nowhere, offering him nothing, nothing to cling to, his guilt for wanting her only making things worse.

I sat on the beach today. I was going to see him but I never got there. I couldn't face him. The sun was hot. The sky was blue. The clouds were fluffy white. People were laughing and having fun. There were boats everywhere, all different sizes and shapes. The sea was dark blue and beautiful and ever so still. There was barely a ripple on the surface. I could see way out across the bay, way out over the water. The buildings there were so clear, like toy building bricks. Everything was perfect. I felt I could walk on the surface, as though nothing could possibly harm me. I couldn't understand it. How could it be? How could it have changed so quickly? How could this water threaten anything?

A rush of anger came up out of me. I was angry at the sun and the sky and the sea and all of the people and I was angry with myself for being so stupidly naive, because I've lived here all my life and I know what the sea can do. I watched my dad leave to go out on it so many times and I watched my mum try to put it all out of her head. I lay in bed and listened to the wind howling and the rain hammering against the window and thought of him out there in it all and tried not to dream of it in my sleep. I woke up enough times to find him sitting on the edge of my bed, stroking my forehead and felt all that relief and happiness. And I experienced the loss, too, listened to him talking to my mum about the night before, listened to all the tiny details, the strange names of the ships and the crews, the places they came from. Sometimes there were visitors, people coming to the house to thank him for what he had done or what he had tried to do, coming to see what he had risked losing. Sometimes I watched them glancing around the room, at my mum and at me, and I saw the sadness in their eyes, how they realised all of that was gone from them now, taken by the water.

Now the water has taken my father.

Listen.

Listen to me.

Let me tell you about not knowing, about waiting and wondering. Let me tell you how it feels to not know where somebody has gone to, when they might come back, if they're going to come back. Let me tell you how it feels to know the truth about something and lie to yourself until your lies become real, and then imagine them shattering like glass into millions of pieces when your fantasy world collapses. How do you pick up those pieces and start to put things back together? How do you even begin?

25

It was on the news and on the radio. There were pictures of Sal's father in the paper. They talked about a hero and then they talked about the villain who'd made the call. They'd traced the call to a telephone box and there was a recording of it played on the TV, the muffled voice of a boy, hurriedly telling the operator his friends had taken a boat and been washed out to sea, the storm raging in the background, somewhere beyond the waves crashing at the shore. JB listened to it all, the darkness rising.

The police came like he knew they would. They were friendly enough and at least they didn't take him to the station. Instead they sat on the bench in the caravan and asked him questions.

'Where were you that night?'

'I was here, in the caravan. Ask my uncle.'

'Did you leave the caravan?'

'No, not until the morning.'

'Have you used the phone box on the beach road?'

'No, never. I've got my mobile. Why? Is that where the call was made from?'

No answer.

'Do you know anything about the emergency call that was made on Thursday?'

'No.'

'Are you sure? We're not saying it was you.'

'Nothing.'

'You have no idea who might have made that call? Not someone you're trying to protect.'

'No. No idea at all.'

'This is a serious business.'

'I know.'

'A man may have died.'

'I know.'

Next morning, the body washed up on the beach down the coast. The discovery meant that Sal was fatherless and that the boy who made the call was responsible.

For two more days JB heard nothing. He had no energy to go to the huts. His uncle made him breakfast and then left him in the caravan. He moped around the place, sometimes walking to the huts and opening the shed, sometimes taking the tins out, before putting them back, locking up and heading back to the caravan to put his head down. His phone was a heavy burden in his pocket, a reminder that he was alone. He sent a text to Carla, then another, but none came back. He tried calling Scooby but got nothing. He got through to his mum but he didn't know what to say to her and he couldn't tell her about what was happening, so he played at things, acted, joked about his uncle's cooking, chatted to Ellie, told her he'd be home soon.

He was sleeping through a morning when there was a commotion outside. He got up to see Moey's gang down in the sea grass behind the huts, hooting and hollering like madmen. The old lady with the cats was watching them from behind twitching curtains.

He pulled on his clothes and went outside. They were away from the path, in the place where the grass was longest. Moey was there, the lad with the bruises, the little lad and Lisette, standing to one side, making most of the noise, shouting at the others.

'Stop it! Leave it alone!'

But whatever it was, Moey and the others were ignoring her, busy instead in their own little world.

JB headed for Lisette. He could see she was frantic, standing in the grass in a short skirt, stepping forward into a patch of nettles and then reversing again, unable to reach the others who had ploughed through the nettles in their trackie bottoms and trainers. She tried again, right foot, left foot, dipping her bare legs tentatively, not getting anywhere, stepping back, jumping up and down on the spot. When she saw JB she turned and ran to him instead, called out to him.

'Make them stop! Please!'

JB looked across at the lads. The three of them were bunched together, their attention focused on the thing beneath them. JB could hear Moey's snarling laughter, the other two laughing with him, urging him on.

'Go on! Wheyyyy! Look at thaaaaat!'

JB clambered through the sea grass. It was stiff and coarse, infiltrated with the nettles that Lisette couldn't overcome. He could see more now. Moey had a lighter and was bent double, flicking it on and off. The little lad had a piece of driftwood and was pressing down on it using his midriff. There was something on the ground beneath them, something living. JB caught a flash of ginger fur.

'Finish it off,' shouted the lad with the bruises.

'Watch this! Watch its fur when I do this!'

'It stinks.'

'Keep it still then!'

JB saw the cat squirm beneath the wood and Moey kick out at it. The cat squeaked pathetically.

'Did you hear that? Hey, listen to this!'

Moey went to kick the cat again. He had his leg in the air when JB bundled into him. He went sprawling into the grass.

'Oi! What the . . . ?'

JB tried levering the wood off the stricken creature but the little lad had the wood firmly in place so that the cat's back legs were trapped under it. The cat's fur was singed and its nose was bloody. The blood had run into its eyes and started to congeal there so that the cat's eyes were hardly open. It tried to struggle free, tore at the wood with its front paws, thrashed its upper body around but the little lad wouldn't relieve the pressure.

'You'll kill it,' shouted JB.

'So what,' said Moey. 'What's your problem?'

'It's a cat,' said JB.

'Never,' sneered Moey. 'Give him a peanut.'

'What's it done to you?'

Moey brushed himself down. He was covered in dry grass seed and pollen.

'Nothing. Why, do you want to take its place?

JB wasn't listening. He spun around and kicked the driftwood, sending it flying out of the little lad's grip. The cat flipped on to its front and darted through the grass like a bullet, straight under the nearest hut.

'Look at it,' said Moey. 'Scared shitless.'

'You're sick.'

'What, like you? Making a hoax call and killing your girlfriend's dad?'

Tomorrow I'm going to say goodbye to my father. I'm not ready to do it but I have to. It feels wrong. It feels like it's happening to someone else. It feels like a mistake.

It gets you in the smallest ways. You can be making a pot of tea and get three cups out instead of two because you've always got three cups out. Sometimes I can be as far as pouring the tea into the cups before I realise what I'm doing. I've seen my mum standing at the bench in the kitchen cutting far too many vegetables for two, seen her stop suddenly when the thought hits her.

The house feels it, too. Sometimes a draught of air sounds like a sigh. Sometimes I walk into a room and something happens to the air, like it doesn't know what to do with this new space that's suddenly been created. The worse place for that is the garage, because that was his place. When I step in there I feel unwelcome. I daren't touch anything, even though everything seems to be crying out to be touched, all the tools just sitting there on the shelves crying out to be used. I leave everything as it is and close the door, let the darkness back in.

I know he wants to see me but I just can't face him. I can't face anybody. There are rumours flying about, that the call was a hoax and that the boat didn't even need to be out. But I don't want to think about that. That would mean that someone was to blame. That would be the same as murder.

And he doesn't know this place. God, it's small enough. If they decide he did it I hate to think what they'll do to him.

Sometimes I feel like he's been sent to me for a reason. I can't explain it to him though. He'd never understand. I don't understand it myself.

I'm talking in riddles.
I'm not making any sense.
Nothing makes any sense any more.

26

JB was up early. When he opened the caravan door a swirl of mist came in at him. He stood on the step looking out at it. It had settled over the caravan site, settled over the marshes. He couldn't see the sea wall and the huts. He could just make out the dark outline of the pylon, hear it humming steadily somewhere above him. For the next half hour he hung around the caravan trying to make himself busy. He made tea and put one steaming mug by his uncle's bed. For once his uncle wasn't the one up and about. He remained under his covers snoring. The dog padded along behind as he paced around. JB took a biscuit from the packet and the dog snapped it up.

He took his mug of tea outside and traipsed through the mist and the sea grass to the huts. His jeans were soaked again but he didn't care. He looked out towards the ocean but there was nothing to see beyond the breakers. The sea and the sky simply folded into one another, the mist heaving and swirling above the shoreline. He looked up and down the line of huts but he could only see two or three clearly. He sipped at his tea until it was too cold and then he threw the rest of it down on to the pebbles. He ran a hand down the wood of the hut in front of him. There was a film of water on the wood. The painting would have to wait until the mist cleared, but that was fine. He wasn't planning on doing any. He was going to the funeral and he didn't care what might happen if Bellows came down to check on him.

He got a message from Lisette. It said that she hated Moey and that she'd never forget what he did to the cat. He didn't know what to send back so he ignored it. He didn't care. But then he thought about the cat, its eyes plastered shut with its own blood, and so he sent a message back to her. He told her that Moey was a coward and that he'd always be a coward and signed it with three XXXs because he knew she'd show it to Moey when he came crawling after her and he wanted Moey to see it. It made him smile to imagine it.

An hour later he was in the alley that cut across the top of the beach and up to the crematorium, the mist still softening everything. He walked past the horses. He could just make them out, two shapes in the grey. They were out in the middle of the meadow, two stone statues. He clicked his tongue at them as he passed but they didn't move and they might easily not have been living at all.

The crematorium was quiet. There was a single light on in the chapel and one car parked outside. He thought about going in but what could he do in there? Instead he stood under the willow tree by the pond, sheltering himself from the mist. He was in his own little world. He pulled his hoodie over his ears to make his world smaller and shoved his hands deep in his pockets. He waited. A fish rose to the surface of the pond and turned over in the water. For a moment he saw the silver scales on its body and the perfect tailfin, then it disappeared back down into the dark pool.

He waited there for thirty minutes while the mist rolled and turned in front of him. He saw pictures in it and his mind drifted. He thought about what might have happened if he'd never got in the car with Scooby, if he'd never seen Haycliffe, never met Moey and his gang, never met Sal, never seen a beach hut.

The funeral hearses came down the hill, two silent black ghosts, making no sound until they turned into the gravel drive. Then there was the crunch of tyres on stone. JB stayed under the willow and sank back into the leaves. He watched as the cars pulled up outside the chapel. More cars were behind, a great line of them. They filled the car park and the roadside beyond the hedge. Sal and her mother emerged from the leading hearse. They walked up to the chapel steps together and then waited at the doorway. Slowly, the rest of the mourners filed into place behind them.

Four men in uniform appeared from the second hearse. They were wearing the formal clothing of the RNLI, each one pristine and perfect. They walked in procession to the first hearse and lifted the coffin to their shoulders. They took the chapel steps one at a time and every move they made spoke of the respect and honour they shared for their lost crew-member.

JB watched Sal. She was stood on the top step. He saw her mother put a hand on her shoulder and he saw Sal lean away from the motion. It surprised him, but now he'd noticed it he noticed other things too, the way Sal was so focused on the coffin, almost ignoring her mother, the way there seemed to be a distance between the two of them. Sal looked alone and desperate, like a swimmer treading water at sea, gasping for breath, slowly drowning.

JB stayed under the willow, watching the men carry the coffin up the steps into the chapel, the mourners filing in behind it, the chapel doors swinging shut, swallowing them up inside.

When they were all gone the feeling of being different came to him again. Sal might have been drowning up there on the steps but he felt as though he were drowning too, fighting and struggling in the water, in a current that wouldn't let go, one that was dragging him further and further away from the shore, further and further out to sea. Nobody was out looking for the boy from the city, the boy from the caravan park, no planes, no helicopters, no boats. Nobody knew of the danger he was in. Nobody cared.

He waited outside the chapel for an hour. The sun broke through the mist and the mist fled so that when the mourners emerged and the procession from the chapel began he could see them blinking and rubbing their eyes against it. Sal appeared, her eyes red and full of tears, her mother behind her, keeping the same distance between them. There was something about Sal, something about her as she stood on the steps and waited for the car to take her away. It was as though half of her were missing, as if she wasn't really there at all. She had been that way since the day on the harbour.

Sal climbed into the lead hearse and it started around the gravel driveway. Too late, he realised it would pass right by the willow tree. He only had time to pull himself back further in to the leaves and try to hide, but as the car passed he found himself staring right at her through the glass. He was caught by a curious image, Sal's face beyond the glass, looking out at him, looking through him, and his own reflection in the glass staring back. It made him think about the night on the train and the boy he'd seen in the window. What would the old JB have done about Sal? None of this. The old JB wouldn't have got himself in this mess. He wanted the old JB back. He wanted him back so badly it hurt. He watched as the car pulled out into the road and took Sal away from him. What was he doing here?

When she was gone, when there was nobody left at all, he walked over the gravel and up the steps. He tried the chapel door. It swung open quietly. Inside there was an impossible stillness. He walked up to another set of doors, hesitated and then pushed them open. The door opened into the chapel of rest. He stood and looked at the cross on the altar and his mind wandered back to his grandad in the chair in the living room, the TV in the corner, his mum coming home from work, the smell of detergent on her clothes, Ellie running in from the bedroom to greet her and then his grandad slumping forwards, the mug of tea in his hand spilling on to his knees, on to the carpet, his mum rushing over to him, Ellie crying, the whole thing happening in five drawn-out seconds that would somehow imprint themselves on his brain for ever more, to demand attention at times like this.

He was back in the alley when they appeared. They were waiting around the corner at the bottom end by the beach. He thought about turning back but they'd already seen him and there was no way he was going to do that once they'd seen him. It didn't matter anyhow. He was ready. Sal had looked through him and that was enough to make him ready. If Moey was looking for a fight then this was a good time.

But Moey wasn't there.

The fat lad was missing too, and Lisette.

The lad with the bruises came up to him.

'Got a message.' He was trying to look tough but there was weakness there and JB smelled it.

'It's from Moey. He says you'd better stop texting Lisette and he says you'd better not say anything. He says if you do he'll make sure they blame you for it.'

'Lisette doesn't care. Not after the other day, and if Moey wants to tell me anything he can tell me himself.'

'Why? Scared?'

'Of you? You're joking. Maybe if I was a kitten . . .'

JB poked at the lad's chest but the lad held his ground.

'They've already traced it to the phone box near you,' said the lad.

'He's got witnesses who say it was you. The voice sounds like you.'

'Yeah? Well, I wasn't there. You were there, you and your lot. I've got witnesses too, people saw you, people heard you talking about it.'

'You ain't got witnesses.'

'The same witnesses that'll have you for the cat. People live on that site, you know. It's not a cemetery.'

He stepped forward and the lad with the bruises backed off. He looked at the others, eyes dancing from face to face, searching for help, but no help came.

'It was Moey,' he said. 'You know it was him.'

'You were there too.'

JB reached the crowd of lads at the bottom of the alley now and the crowd parted like a wave in front of him.

'You tell Moey about the witnesses. Tell him about the camera too if you want.'

The lad with the bruises shouted after him.

'There ain't no camera.'

JB nodded and made like he was taking a photo. Two of the lads pulled their hoodies up and turned their faces away. JB laughed.

'Look at you all,' he shouted. 'You wouldn't last two minutes over there.'

He swung his arms in the direction of the lego-brick tower blocks sitting on the horizon and then he made off up the sea wall, striding onwards. He was buzzing, huge rushes of adrenalin pounding through his veins and he felt he could take on the whole world.

27

Back at the caravan he lay listening to the radio, a plate of chips on the bed beside him. He'd made them when he got back, his hands busy for something to do, and then he'd hardly touched them. He closed his eyes and pictured her face as the car drove her away and tried to block the picture out, but the moment he did it started searching for a way back in again. He knew if he could find sleep he'd be all right. Sleep was the safest place of all. But sleep would not come to him.

When the knock came he was almost out of it. It simply filled a part of his daydream, but when it came a second time it woke him. He rolled off the bed and opened the door. He was expecting the woman with the cats or even Bellows, but it was Sal.

'Will you come with me?'

'Where to?'

'Just come,' she said.

At first they walked in silence, down through the sea grass to the huts. When they got there she led him past them. As they walked she counted each one.

'Seventy-five,' she said, when they reached the last hut he'd painted.

'Twelve to go,' he said.

'How long will that take?'

'Another few weeks, I suppose.'

'Then what?'

'Dunno. But there's no way I'm starting at the first one again.'

She laughed then. Her face filled with colour and her eyes brightened and suddenly, for a moment, the darkness was obliterated by the light. She reached out and took his hand.

When they reached hut seventy-seven she stopped.

'Will you paint ours blue?' she asked. 'Blue like the sky.'

He thought about what his uncle had told him, about missing it out and not touching it. But things had changed.

He nodded.

'Come on,' she said. 'It's a long way yet . . .'

'Where are we going?'

'You'll see,' she said.

They walked as far as the reserve. He'd been there before, way back when he first arrived. He'd spent the whole time talking to Carla on his mobile and he'd not taken any of it in then. He'd simply reached the gate, stopped and gone back. This time Sal pulled the gate open and held it for him. There was hardly room to squeeze past her and when he did, he felt a surge of need rush through him. He wanted to hold her but he couldn't, not today. Not like this. Instead he carried on walking. She trotted up to him and took his hand.

'I saw you today,' she said. 'Under the willow tree.'

'Yeah,' he said. 'You looked . . . lost.'

She walked on without saying anything.

'I didn't make the hoax call,' he said.

'I know,' she said.

'How do you know?' he asked.

'Don't talk about it,' she said. 'I just know, that's all.'

They crossed the reserve, feet crunching on the tiny pebbles, stepping between the flowers and plants. She was only partly with him. Another part of her was concentrated on the water.

'You're looking for that place again . . .'

'Shhh. You have to concentrate.'

On they went, him thinking about how his hand felt in hers and her staring at the waterline. There was nothing to see. Just the water, still and flat, the afternoon sunlight shimmering magically upon it, but there was no magical ships' graveyard, no escape from what was real.

'I asked my uncle about it,' said JB. 'He said he's heard about it but you'll never find it if you go looking for it.'

'I've heard that too,' she said. 'But if you can't find it when you look for it what's the point of it being anywhere?'

She stopped.

'Maybe it knows,' she said. 'Maybe it senses we're here and it's hiding.'

'Why would it hide?'

'So we don't tell anybody where to find it.'

'Maybe,' he said, but he was struggling to keep up with her, finding it more and more difficult not to drag her away before she lost herself completely. They were looking for something that didn't exist.

Late afternoon, the air in the caravan stale. JB had the curtain across in case his uncle came in. She was leaning against his shoulder, her soft skin against his, speaking but not to him, just getting the words out. He was stroking her hair. He'd been doing this for half an hour.

'I had a row with Mum,' she said. 'I know that's bad on a day like this but she . . . we're so different. It was like she wanted to put on a show. There were camera crews outside our house this morning. Can you believe that? She gave them permission to be there. I don't understand her.'

'At the chapel, I wanted to walk in after you,' he said. 'I wanted to shout at the lot of them and tell them. Not just about your dad but about the huts and about my uncle, about the way they stuck the blame on me.'

'They'd have murdered you,' she said. 'They do it because it's easy, easier to blame a stranger or an outsider than it is to blame one of their own. If it's one of their own that's a problem they helped cause. My dad did it all the time, blamed the holiday-makers and day-trippers, blamed the school they sent me to, blamed the lifeboat station up the coast at East Bay whenever a shout went bad.'

'My mum says the estate's like that now. When she was younger people used to look out for each other but now they only look out for themselves. She says the minute something goes wrong they look for someone to blame. Even when it's their own kids they blame someone else's. That's why she sent me down here. She says the estate's poisonous and I'm better off out of it. But they should have let me stay. They should have let me do something like this beach hut thing up there. The whole place is a mess. It needs a lick of paint. I could have done that. We painted the community centre once, a whole gang of us. They let us tag it and everything. Then the council blokes came and whitewashed it all out. Part of some clean-up thing they were doing. We used to have a boxing ring in the community centre. Everybody went down there and got into boxing. It was great. Then there was a fight outside and some lad got put in hospital. After that they shut the boxing club down. They said it caused the fight. But it didn't. This guy showed us how to train and what to eat and how to concentrate. I was buzzing when I came out of there. Three times a week it was, then just like that it closed. That's what we got sick of, getting into something new and then losing it. We all just gave up. We did our own thing.'

'There was a youth club here,' she said. 'I never went because Dad wouldn't let me. He said it attracted the wrong crowd. Once I tried going but word got back to him and I was grounded for a week. It's not there any more. I think it's an art gallery or something.'

His mind drifted elsewhere now, recalling the way his hands had slipped behind her, the feel of the sweat in the small of her back, the sound of her breathing as he kissed her shoulders, the way she'd pulled him to her . . .

She was talking about her father.

'Every time the phone rang last week I rushed to answer it and hoped for news and every time it was somebody who didn't have any news, somebody calling to wish us well and to make sure we were coping, someone offering help. My mum kept taking the phone from me and telling them how grateful we both were, how we were still hoping for everything to be okay, that we had to because hope was all we had left. But the people making the calls, they knew there was no hope, just like we knew there was no hope. It was all a game.'

. . . the smell of her . . .

'It was his duty. That was all that mattered to him. His duty. It made him who he was. He never questioned it. Neither did my mum. I think she wanted to but she didn't. He wouldn't talk about it, ever. There was no chance of him quitting, no matter how dangerous things got. It was just part of our lives.'

. . . the touch of her fingers, the way she'd held him, dug her fingernails into his back, the ferocity of it, of being inside her, the warmth . . .

'I keep thinking about the last time I saw him. We had dinner and I went into the lounge to watch TV. He shouted something about the TV programme I was watching and went out to the garage and I didn't really hear him properly and I didn't want interrupting so I pretended not to hear. That was the last thing he said to me. I don't even remember what the programme was. Some rubbish.'

. . . the heat building . . . and the fear too, the fear of being a disappointment, the way that feeling had come to him and how he'd tried to control it . . .

'I'm so far out of it all I can't explain it. I can't get to grips with how I've ended up like this. What do I do now, Jay? What do I do now that he's dead? Mum's not coping. She'll do something stupid. I just know she will. I've got to look after her . . . and I really thought we'd find that place today. I really thought the sea would give it up just to make amends. But I couldn't even have that. My dad's dead and I can't find a few ships on a beach. Why?'

. . . as she stiffened under him, made tiny noises in her throat . . . the way their bodies shook and how she'd held on to him as it happened so that it was like they were one living thing . . . one living breathing thing that would cope because they were stronger than all the stuff that was coming at them, much stronger, stronger than anything. He'd believed it. He still believed it, but she was shaking again, with tears this time, so it was hard to believe anything at all. He held her in the darkness, rocked her in his arms, whispered in her ear.

'You'll be okay,' he said. 'We'll be okay. We'll show them. We'll show them. We'll show them.'

He said it over and over until he felt her drift away and then he sat there in the darkness, holding the covers over her, not worrying about the chill on his skin, not caring about it, repeating the words to himself until he almost believed them to be true.

When he woke the caravan was dark. The space beside him was empty. He jumped up and opened the door, looked out at the site, the other caravans' grey shapes in the gloom, the lights of the beach road leading his eye back towards the town.

He retreated, back to his bed, lay with his head on the pillow, breathed in the scent of her, a scent already beginning to weaken.

28

Twelve more huts.

Eleven.

Ten.

Nine.

Eight.

The days passing. No sign. No signal. Just the huts and the paint. Nothing coming from her. Nothing coming his way. Nothing from Moey's gang either.

The ocean and the birds, the empty marshes, his uncle in the evenings, the two of them silently eating or talking quietly in front of the TV, sometimes playing cards, the nights passing by painfully slowly, his mobile blinking away but receiving no message, a heartbeat weakening.

29

Seven huts remaining. He set off to meet her, cut through the alley. The black horse was in the field, hiding in the shadows of the trees, but the grey horse was nowhere to be seen.

He found her on the grass slopes. She'd agreed to be there but the call had been awkward and at first she'd not wanted to come. It was all he could do to get her to talk to him.

'Shut up,' she said. 'Just shut up and don't speak. Don't spoil it. I want to be with you without knowing you. I want to imagine you instead. It's better that way. Trust me. I want to take things easy. I want to drift.'

So he sat there next to her, waiting, staring over the slopes and out at the water, wishing he'd never called, wishing it could all be over, fearing the same.

'Listen,' she said at last. 'You know what I think? All of this stuff is happening for a reason.'

He laughed. He couldn't help himself.

'Why are you laughing?'

'I don't believe in all that stuff. Reasons. Master plans. What if you want to fight for something? What if you want to change something? You can control things. It's not all mapped out.'

'Then you fight to control it and it becomes a reason. It's the same.'

'That's just twisting things to suit.'

'So? What's wrong with that?'

'There's too many maybes. Like maybe if I hadn't come here your dad would still be alive.'

'Maybe. But you did and . . .'

'Sorry. I didn't mean that.'

'It's okay. It's true. We met for a reason. I believe it even if you don't. You were sent to me for a reason.'

'What? I was meant to come here, to this place because you needed it . . . ?'

'Yes . . . to help . . . and you were there when I needed you, but . . .'

'But?'

'Now . . .'

'Now?'

'Now things are different. I need to sort Mum out. I need to sort me out.'

'Then what about me?'

'What about you?'

'Where are my reasons? How do I fit in?' He mocked her now, anger boiling inside. 'Oh, don't worry about Jay. He got his ASBO. He got sent away. But he'll be all right. He'll survive. He's strong. And if not, so what? It's only Jay. Just some loser.'

He hated himself even as the words came out. He couldn't believe this was happening, that they were talking to each other like this. He couldn't believe he'd waited to see her and now here he was acting like a child. There was a moment when his words were suspended in the air in front of them, somewhere between the sea wall and the water. He tried to grab them back but a gust of wind carried them away.

'I've got to go,' she said.

'Go now?'

'It's getting late. Mum will be wondering. She's not the same . . .'

'I'm sorry,' he said. 'I didn't mean it . . .'

'It doesn't matter,' she said. 'You don't have to be sorry. You're right. But I still have to go.'

She jumped down off the wall. She didn't move to kiss him and he couldn't bring himself to go after her. He watched her walk away from him. He was caught again, caught between himself and her, between his needs and hers. He felt selfish for turning the conversation around to his needs but how long was he meant to go on not having any needs? How long could somebody be happy when their needs were relegated to the dustbin? A month? Three months? A year? A lifetime?

He tried to understand, wanted so much to understand, but in truth he didn't understand a word. What he was hearing were excuses, the same excuses he'd always heard. All he knew was that it frightened him. A part of him was leaving. He was chasing it already. Chasing it blindly, with panting breath, but he couldn't catch it. It was already out of sight. She had sucked it out of him and spewed it into the rubbish that marked the high-water line. He would have to go crawling and picking through it all to find that part of himself again, if it could be found, if it wasn't lost for ever.

A football rolled towards him. When he looked up a small boy was staring back at him. JB picked the ball up and kicked it, watched the boy try to catch it and miss, watched it roll down the slope and off the wall where it bounced twice on the promenade before dropping to the beach. The boy went after it.

JB dropped down off the wall too. He started back for the caravan, anger still raging inside. It was white-hot and impossible to control. He kicked a pebble from the path, watched it flick up over the wall and crack against the window frame of one of the houses. Seconds later a man came out of a doorway.

'What the hell do you think you're doing?' he shouted.

This was his life. It had always been this way, just one slice of bad luck after another. If he let himself believe in her ideas about reasons, he may as well walk into the sea until it swallowed him.

'You'll bloody well pay if it's broken . . .' shouted the man, but JB wasn't listening, not really. He was thinking instead, about all of the moments like this, each one stacked up on top of each other. He was an idiot for expecting her to understand. How could she understand, her with her house on the hill? The differences between them were growing, each new thing adding to the last, forcing a separation that would eventually carry her clear of him.

Reasons. One thing was certain. Any reasons would be out to get him. That's what reasons did. They trapped like a tide. The only way to avoid them was to submerge yourself fully, find the bottom and hold on to something, fight the current, stop it carrying you away.

30

He missed her more as each day passed. He got up early, sat on the caravan steps and sipped at his tea. The dog came over and flopped down beside him. He knew he had to keep busy. It was no use thinking about it all over and over and over again. He still had seven huts left and that meant seven days until he was finished. Bellows would come back and realise the game was up. He'd start making other plans. Bellows might send him away. There was no doubt he wanted to wash his hands clean of it all. JB thought about slowing down, but that was no good because then he had times like these to deal with. It was bad enough when it rained and he was forced to hang around the caravan kicking his heels.

He was terrified they'd send him somewhere else one day and she would come the next day, find him gone and then he'd never know. He had to see her one more time, to say everything that should have been said.

For the last days he developed a new routine. It began with the tea on the steps. He'd feed the dog and then wade through the sea grass and paint. At eleven he'd return to the caravan and make a sandwich. He'd paint again until three, slowly, lazily, taking more care now with the finish than he'd ever done.

The worst part still lay ahead of him, though. That's when he had to be careful. It was too easy to get sidetracked, too easy to sit around for hours thinking. Thinking, he learned, was the problem. He worked on his lyrics, tried to include his feelings without getting carried away. He'd think back to the city, to his friends, to the things that had happened, and he'd try to build pictures up and rhyme them together. As long as he was in the city she couldn't get to him. He hadn't known her then. She had no face. She was just a shadow, something that might happen in a future time and place, something that existed in a fantasy moment and could never be real.

His uncle would come back in the evening and they'd eat anything from a can and toast. His uncle would chuck a pan on the stove and half an hour later they'd be through with it. Sometimes they talked but mostly they ate in silence. His uncle was familiar with things being that way and JB came to appreciate the same. His uncle would disappear again then, to the allotment mostly, leaving him enclosed in darkness. This was the worst time, waiting for tiredness, waiting for sleep. No matter how he tried she would come to him then. His head might settle on a subject that wasn't her, might sit there a while, but all too soon she would move in and push the subject to one side. By the time his eyes closed there was only her in his head.

Sleep was the only relief. For some reason she couldn't get into his dreams any more. They were his only escape from any of it and he knew that if she found a way into the place where his dreams were stored there would be no escaping her, ever.

31

Saturday. High summer. Three huts to go.

Four days had passed. Despite his routine he was going crazy with it all. He went into town and walked around, searching for her. He wanted to run into her. He wanted to make it look like an accident. He didn't have the courage to go to her. He couldn't bring himself to do it. In his head was the fear that she might truly not want to see him. He couldn't face that. He walked through the town, looking in shop windows, trying to fake an interest in things that held no interest. The town was busy with tourists, families mostly but sickeningly couples too, walking hand in hand, smiling, sometimes laughing out loud. He hated them. The pubs were full of people, some spilling out on to the street, slopping lager on the pavement. He barged through the crowds, sweating inside his hoodie, ignoring them when they shouted at him. The ice-cream parlours were brimming with flustered parents and impatient children. A line of cars sat in the road in the heat. Kids looked out at him from behind the windows and made faces. They had buckets and spades on their laps. He wanted to scream at them, at everybody. He wanted to be alone, but that would mean going back to the caravan and sitting around waiting with no chance of seeing her. That would be unbearable. So he remained outside and contained it all in the hope that they might meet somehow.

But he couldn't find her. He went to the sea front and to the grass slopes where they used to meet, back when everything had been easy between them. He sat down in a quiet place and took his hoodie off, revelling in the sunlight. He surveyed the beach from above and waited in hope. He thought she might even come to the slopes herself, answering a calling like he had.

The beach was packed. He watched a group of teenagers, girls and lads together, the lads lithe and trimmed, full of themselves. He was nothing like them. The girls were self-conscious on the beach, but full of confidence in the water. They bathed in the blue water, leaned towards each other and whispered, shared secrets. He looked for her amongst them. They were her kind. They would know her. They were probably her friends. Perhaps they were whispering about him, pointing him out, laughing at his stupidity.

The lads tried something. They clambered up on to the breakwater and dived off. The girls screamed as the lads made bigger and bigger splashes. It was a contest to see who could impress the most. He watched the bravest climb on to the breakwater and turn his back on his friends. With a spring the lad performed a back flip and landed gracefully in the water. The others cheered. He did it again. One of his friends climbed up to have a go but then lost his nerve and bombed into the sea instead, fooling the girls, causing more screams. The back-flip boy tried for a third time. He perched himself on the breakwater, demanding attention, but this time his feet slipped half-way through and he didn't gain enough distance. His head cracked against the breakwater. The girls screamed again as his body flipped in an impossible way, but now the screams were different. The lad came up with his head in his hands. When he pulled his hands away they were covered in blood. It covered the front of his body and shone in the sunlight. His friends waded to his aid. They helped him up on to the beach, sat him down and gave him a towel. He tried to wave them away but nobody was listening to him. Some of the adults on the beach came over to help. The towel was a soaking wet rag of red. They had to give him another and immediately a new spot started growing. A lifeguard, splashed in yellow and red colours, came sprinting down the beach. He led the boy and his friends up the beach and away towards the lifeguard point, the boy weak-legged now, his skin much paler than the others. The crowd slowly dispersed. Some people next to JB were talking about it all. He looked over at them and grimaced. They grimaced back.

'I said that would happen,' said a fat woman in a leopard-skin bikini. 'It was bound to happen eventually.'

He nodded then turned away and looked down at the beach again. A group of children were hunting crabs in the shallows by the break-water, oblivious to the drama. He saw one little girl pick up a medium-sized crab and hold it out in front of her. The crab's pincers waved frantically in the air. The little girl dropped it into a purple bucket. Another little girl went over to her and peered inside. She put her fingers tentatively into the bucket of water then withdrew her hand and gave a shrill cry. He wondered if the crab had bitten her.

There was action everywhere. A group of teenagers came scooting along the promenade on skateboards. They ignored the painted sign that read 'No cycling or skateboarding'. Nobody seemed to care. Older people were splayed out on towels and in deck chairs, drinking from flasks, watching the children with dutiful eyes. People were sat on the verandahs of their beach huts eating fish and chips from plastic cartons. Summer had arrived early. People were using the beach huts on his beach already, even though they were meant to wait another week. Maybe next year he'd get to paint the huts up this way. Maybe it would become his life. Or maybe he'd be blamed for the hoax call and never be allowed to set foot in the town again.

He trotted down to the beach and started along it. He saw one boy all on his own, the same boy who had kicked the football at him on the day he'd last seen Sal. Without thinking too much he leapt off the promenade on to the beach. His feet slid away from him as he made his way over the stacked pebbles. The small boy looked around when he got closer then went back to whatever he was doing. JB settled himself on the stones and waited. The boy was poking at something with a stick. When he looked up a second time, he mumbled, 'Hello.'

'You're not catching crabs then?' JB asked him.

'It's cruel,' said the boy.

'I saw what that crab did to the girl,' said JB. 'It wasn't messing around.'

'For the crabs,' said the boy. 'Cruel for the crabs. I don't care what happens to her. She's been chucking crabs into that bucket all afternoon. The water must be boiling by now. She's probably cooking those crabs alive. And all the crabs are different sizes. She doesn't have a clue. All the big ones will get to the top and all the little ones will sink to the bottom. It's no fun being a little crab in that bucket of hers.'

'You take crabs seriously,' he said.

'Sometimes,' said the boy. 'It's cruel though, when you do it wrong like she is.'

JB nodded.

'Where's your girlfriend?' the boy asked.

'Who?'

'Your girlfriend. The girl with the long hair. You always sit up there with her. I've seen you loads of times.'

'Oh, she's not my girlfriend,' he said.

'Did you break up?' asked the boy.

'She was never my girlfriend.'

The boy shook his head. Now he was throwing pebbles at a can half-buried in the ground in front of them. Sometimes his pebbles bounced and hit it.

The boy pointed. 'It doesn't count if it bounces first. You have to hit it full on.'

JB picked up a hand full of pebbles and started firing them at the target.

'It's not easy,' he said.

The boy laughed.

'It's not meant to be,' said the boy. 'I keep moving it so it gets harder and harder.'

For a while they said nothing, just threw the pebbles at the can.

'She's not my girlfriend, you know,' JB said.

'You said already,' said the boy.

'Well then,' he said. 'You haven't seen her all day? What about yesterday or the day before?'

'I haven't seen her for ages,' said the boy.

There were stones bouncing in all directions. A stone from the boy's hand went hurtling through the air, striking the can full on. It skittled over the pebbles and came to rest even further away.

'I win,' said the boy.

'I didn't know it was a contest,' he said.

'Of course it's a contest,' said the boy. 'Now we see who can hit it again.'

He felt strangely relaxed with the boy. He felt he could say anything and not be heard. It was like being with his uncle's dog. It was a way to get things out of himself and not worry about it. They continued to throw pebbles in their little competition. Each time one of them hit the can the boy would get up and move it further away until it was an effort just to reach it.

32

Plates empty on the table, a light breeze coming in through the caravan door cooling the place. JB came out with it.

'What did Jefferies mean when he called you a murderer?'

His uncle lifted his eyes from the plate in front of him.

'You want to talk about that?'

JB nodded.

His uncle gave a little nod, shrugged his shoulders.

'Some people only hear what they want to hear,' he sighed. 'It's as simple as toast. I learned that in the hardest way possible and now you're learning it too. It's the old Bridge curse. Your aunt used to laugh about it until it happened, then she saw the other side of it and it put an end to her. Poor woman. They killed her, Jay, with their lies and gossip.'

'So it's lies, then? Nobody died.'

'No. No, that's the truth. Two people died on my boat. But they didn't die in the way everybody says they did and they didn't die because of anybody. They just died.'

'How?'

'How did Sal's father die? Nobody will ever really know. Perhaps he didn't tie himself on properly. Perhaps he slipped at just the wrong moment. Perhaps he made a bad decision.'

JB interrupted.

'How?' he asked.

'A storm came in quicker than we expected, caught us in the channel. The nets got twisted around the propeller, put us at the mercy of the weather. Two men in my crew tried to get the nets free. They were worried we'd lose the catch and they were worried we'd lose the gear. Losing the catch was one thing but if we'd lost the gear the boat would have been out of action for weeks. Anyway, they went on deck and the sea took them.'

'So why did you get the blame?'

'Because people don't like accidents, especially fishing accidents. It's a dangerous job and everybody knows it, but nobody wants to admit how dangerous it is, not to their families and not to themselves. If they can blame somebody for an accident they will. That way, when the men go out they think they have control over what's going to happen. You can have so much control, but there's a limit. You can't control the sea. You curse it, you fight it, sometimes you even love it, but you never ever control it. Any man who works at sea knows that. But if you think someone's to blame when things go wrong, well then it's so much easier getting on that boat the next time. It's kidology, but it works.'

He paused.

'I never was the most popular bloke on the harbour. I wasn't a true local. But I was good at locating the catch. I had a kind of sixth sense. So here were all these blokes who'd grown up in the town and knew the water since they were kids and there was me. But it's an industry, so if you work hard enough and keep on bringing the fish in sooner or later somebody will see they're missing out on a good thing. A couple of the fishmongers took a chance with me. I earned the respect of the fishermen and a truce settled. Or that's what I thought. Stayed that way for years until the accident, but the two men on my boat were local and when they were lost all the old divisions opened up.

'I went out on the water a few times after the accident but it was hard to get crew. I'd get someone for a day and then turn up the next day to find them on someone else's boat. They were taking these guys on just to stop me using them. People stopped buying my fish. I was out of business in a month. A net came down and swept me away, just like that.'

He looked JB in the eye.

'There was nothing I could do. When everybody's against you there's not much one person can do except get out of there and try to find a place. I went to your grandad's for a while but I didn't like it. It just reminded me why I'd left the city in the first place. I settled out here and kept out of their way. After a while one or two people came to see me on the quiet, said they knew it wasn't my doing but that it was hard to speak up about it. I knew what they meant. They had their own livelihoods to think about. They helped me get set up with the site maintenance and the allotments. It's enough. There are just people like Jefferies to put up with from time to time.'

His uncle shook his head.

'He's got a wife and daughter,' he said. 'I feel for them. It's a terrible thing when the sea takes a soul.'

JB didn't hear the last bit. He was stuck on the word 'daughter' and he couldn't move beyond it.

That night, another dream.

He had a lighter in one hand and a deodorant can in the other and he was spraying the deodorant over the flame to make a flamethrower, chasing Carla around the kiddies' playground, sending bursts of fire shooting into the darkness.

On the roundabout he sat and let them spin him, shooting the flame and leaving a trail behind, like those photographs where they leave the exposure running. Scooby came up with the petrol can from his old bike. JB was happy making lines but Scooby was taking it further, tipping petrol on the scrub and throwing lit matches into it, letting the flames burn themselves out. He poured some on one of the swings next and lit that so that when he pushed the swing there was an arc of light. The plastic seat melted but nobody looked at it for long. They were looking at Scooby. He started spinning the roundabout until JB had to jump off and when it was really spinning he leaned over it and poured the rest of the petrol.

'For my final trick! Stand clear ladies and geezers . . .'

'Don't put that much on . . .'

Too late.

He lit the match and threw it on to the roundabout, sending flames in circles, a spinning, gyrating light show. Carla told him to put it out but there was no getting near it. The flames died but black smoke came out instead as the rubbish inside the structure started to burn. JB tried to grab the metal handle and stop it spinning but it was too hot to touch. There was no water anywhere. Flames started to lick up from inside. The wooden slats caught alight and that was the signal for them to scatter, out into the alleyways, their feet slapping on the pavement, shouting and screaming, hearing the sound of the fire engine out on the parkway, seeing the flashing lights as it pulled into the estate.

The dream ended with the roundabout a sodden black skeleton, no use to anyone. The police stuck some blue tape around it but somebody tore the tape away and wrapped it around a car for a joke.

33

He set off on foot, across the marshes, following the pylons, just as they had on the day it all happened. As he walked he tried to picture the day in his mind, the moment they first touched each other in play, the moment they took each other by the hand, the silence between them, the moment they stopped to look back in the direction they had come, the moment she leaned in and kissed him. He tried to put himself in the exact spot where each of these things happened, creating a map in his mind, tracing his way back there, to the nature reserve, to the very place where he'd felt his whole being slip into her possession.

Birds skimmed low across the flat marshland, common gull, herring gull, black-backed gull, names he had learned from Sal. They rose up on the air currents and disappeared from his view beyond the sea wall. He listened to the raucous calls of the bigger birds, the peeps and chucks of the smaller birds. He listened to the buzz of the insects, the gentle rhythmic accompaniment of the sea. He trained all of his senses into searching for every memory, stopped to gauge the temperature of his surroundings, waited for it to be right, and walked on once more. In this way he would find the graveyard and there he would find his answer, amidst the skeletons of the boats, amidst the ghosts.

The sun was low in the sky. He felt extremely close, so close he could feel its presence, but when he climbed the sea wall and looked out across the beach there was just the shingle shore, the wispy grasses and bright flowers, the flat sea beyond. He looked over at the horizon and tried to gain some perspective but it was all the same to him, impossible to identify one point from another.

He gave up on the marshes then and jumped down from the sea wall on to the pebbles. He was on the nature reserve now. He couldn't remember if they had wandered on to the reserve that day, but another part of him nagged and nagged until he felt that perhaps they had. Perhaps the secret to finding the place was the reserve. Perhaps the reserve helped to keep others away. Perhaps they had been so engrossed in each other that they had wandered aimlessly. It was true, they had.

The sky was empty, the light of the day fading blue to pink. Here in the solitude of the reserve, all was quiet. His heart started to race. He could feel it in his chest, pounding violently. His breath quickened. He was close. Something inside him started to twist and stretch his nerves so that he felt pain too, a searing pain behind the eyes. Was his body trying to warn him? He scoured the reserve for a sign, a piece of wreckage, driftwood, the tip of a mast, anything, but there was just the grass and the flowers, the land and the water.

A bird shot up out of a patch of kale in front of him. It screeched and circled above, dived, coming close, protecting its young, sent him scurrying away across the beach, his concentration gone, his nerves spent.

A chill surged through him then and he recognised a new feeling. He was unwelcome in this place. It didn't want him. The air had turned colder, the breeze coming in straight off the sea, straight off the water, which looked choppier now. His skin tightened and pimples appeared up his arms. The sky blackened above him.

When the thought came to him, it came in such a way that all of his insides felt hollowed out, as though a ferocious creature had gutted him.

You'll never find it if you go looking for it.

He turned and looked back along the coast towards the town. Lights were twinkling in the dusk. The earliest stars were visible above. He stood and watched the light drain from the day and the last embers of comfort drain with it.

All was silent. All was still.

Darkness was coming to the marshes. There was nothing to see, nothing to discover, nothing to tell him that any of it had been real. All he had was memories. He wanted to leave them behind here, bury them in the shingle and let the sea break them up and carry them away, grain by grain. But the sea didn't want them. He was stuck with them, pictures of moments that would spring up unannounced, catch him out, tease and play with him at will.

And that's when it appeared, silent shapes in the gloom ahead, taking on one form, altering, fluctuating, becoming something and then shifting to nothing, dark shadows and silhouettes, a broken mast, a ripped hull, a punctured bow, a torn-off stern, the rudder clinging perilously to it. He was surrounded by a terrible feeling of pain and suffering, of heartbreak, despair and loss. The wind picked up and whistled through the wreckage, lost souls calling out, high-pitched and desperate, a choir of ghosts.

This was the place she'd longed for. He had found it without her. It had showed itself because it recognised him, recognised his desperation and he knew he had to get away from it, otherwise it would trap him here, keep him prisoner forever.

He turned and ran up the beach, not daring to look behind him.

When he reached the sea wall he jumped on to it and stared at the town, at the hill, tried to make out her house amongst so many. He told himself she would have memories too, moments that would turn her insides out, moments that would bring pain, moments like this. And he wanted to tell her he'd found the place, found it just where she'd been looking. He wanted to see her face light up as she saw he was telling the truth, but he knew, even as he thought it, that he was lying to himself because she wouldn't believe him. She'd think it was an excuse. She'd think he wasn't beyond doing or saying anything to see her and then she'd begin to hate him, for not letting go. And even if she did believe him, how could he describe it to her? How could he describe the feelings it had caused in him? How could he describe the terror of it without turning her against him, explain to her that the ships' graveyard was the last place she'd want her father's memory to be laid to rest, that he'd never rest there, only suffer for all eternity?

34

Sunday evening saw him working on the last hut (red). He made a final stroke with the brush, joining the two sections of newly painted wood to create one continuous red block that glistened when he stepped back and let the sun fall upon it.

His work was done. He carried the tin and the brush to the storage shed, cleaned the brush down and locked the shed behind him.

His head was a mixture of thoughts, occupied by what had gone and what was to come. He had one more concrete thing to do. He took the lyrics from his back pocket and read them again.

> Lost at sea
> Beyond the debris
> Searching for a signal
> Battery power low
> A single satellite
> Trapped in the flow

Lost at sea
Drifting here
Beyond the horizon
Soon to disappear

They weren't worth very much but he had written them for Sal and now he had to give them to her. At dusk he walked along the beach and up the alley for the last time, but when he reached her gate he found it impossible to move another muscle. He was scared that he would look into her eyes and see nothing and he could not overcome it. Instead, he crept around the side of the house. The back lawn was flooded with light from the living-room window. He dropped to his knees below the glass and then slowly, slowly inched his way up until he could see inside. She was sat at the piano. She had her back to him, was sitting straight and perfect on the stool. He could see her shoulders, the texture of her skin. He wanted more than anything to reach out and touch her. He put his hands on the sill for balance and some of the paint flaked away in his fingers.

He crept back to the front of the house and quietly dropped the lyric sheet through the letterbox, feeling foolish as he did but doing it anyway. Back at the gate he took one last look at the house, at the big front door and the evenly spaced windows. The difference between them was here in front of him and if he ever forgot he only had to stand in this place and look to see the truth.

He walked back to the beach and sat on the sea wall until the stars were clear and bright in the black sky, and then he got up and made his way back to the site. He stopped twice to look back at the lights of the coast road and followed them with his eyes, to the mass of lights that made up the town, followed the line that led up the hill. By counting the street lights he could almost work out where her road began and from there the very street light outside her bedroom window. But he couldn't be sure he had it right. He couldn't direct his feelings toward her for fear of missing and sending them towards the wrong destination. Things like this had haunted him all summer.

He was ploughing through the sea grass when he noticed the patrol cars outside the caravan. He ducked down and retreated, knowing they were here to bring him in for the hoax call, meaning to hide at the huts until they'd gone, but there was a fire burning on the beach by the huts. Moey's gang were huddled around it. He could hear their laughter. He watched as Moey stood and poured petrol on the flames. The gang cheered and laughed and broke up, scattered on the shoreline looking for driftwood, then they settled as the flames settled and went back to their huddle, became one whole being once more.

I need to know what a person is prepared to do for me, how far they're prepared to go. Dad went to places for me but he went to places for others too and now he's gone some place where nobody can reach him for help of any kind.

People let you down. It happens all the time. When you need somebody to listen, when it's really obvious that you need help, that's the acid test. Forget the other times. I'm talking about somebody being there and listening to what I have to say, even though they'd rather be somewhere else, even if they've got things they want to say, things that they're worried about. It's a lot to ask. Some people come through it and some people don't.

I want him to understand. I want him to know what I'm going through and I think he does but it's not fair on him because he's not to blame and it's not fair because he wants to talk about us and there can't be an us, not now, not ever. I'm so tired, so tired of thinking about it all. All I want to do is sleep, to wrap up warm and cosy in my duvet and spend a whole day doing nothing, a week, a month, a year even.

Mum is the opposite. She's just becoming busier with each day. Busier and busier. She doesn't want to talk. She has no time to listen. I don't know where she's heading.

I crept upstairs to the front bedroom tonight and looked down on the yard. I saw him there. I didn't want to speak to him. I couldn't. I had nothing to say. He was going to want to talk about the day we shared. He'd want some explanation, some reason, and some idea of how I felt about it. I didn't have any of that to give. I had to hide and wait for him to go away. That's just how I felt.

Asboville

I sat in the darkness and listened for the sound of the waves down on the shore. They came to me. They washed over all the other sounds and told me not to worry and they said my dad was with them and that he loved me and that he'd be waiting for me and that he understood it was time for me to do the things I'd talked about and be strong enough to get away from the town and to do it now before it was too late. I'm going to do it too. It's my life. I control it. I do what I want to do.

35

He waited in the grass for another minute and then broke cover, marched over to the gang, heading straight for Moey. When Moey saw him coming he got to his feet.

'Not with your girlfriend then . . .'

Moey grinned.

'Or has she dumped you? Not surprising seeing as you killed her dad.'

JB faced up to him in the firelight. The lad with the bruises and the little lad came up behind.

'What you gonna do?' said Moey.

JB took a breath.

'Nothing,' said Moey. 'Because you've got an ASBO that says you have to stay out of trouble. And you do just what it tells you like a good little boy . . .

'Thing is, I don't think you could do anything anyway. I reckon you're a fake.'

It shouldn't have mattered that Moey was cavorting around him. He knew better but it got to him all the same. Moey went through his routine, stepping this way and that, grinning from ear to ear. The lad with the bruises grinned too.

'This place is nothing,' said JB. 'It's just a scummy little pond for you to swim around in. I've done it where it counts. You haven't got a clue.'

Moey tilted his head back and JB saw the tell-tale look in his eyes. He was weighing up the situation, unsure which way was best. The little lad took a step backwards. Moey grinned again.

'ASBO,' he said. 'A-S-B-O. You think that makes you special. But it doesn't. It means you were stupid enough to get caught, that's all. I should have one. I should have the biggest ASBO there is. I want a poster with my face on.'

'You can have that,' said JB. 'Just own up about the hoax call.'

'Yeah right,' said Moey. 'That's murder, that is. You can keep that.'

JB looked past him and out towards the ocean. Way off on the horizon he could see the towers, the lights blinking back at him. He'd come all this way over the water and somehow it had all followed him, all the trouble, all the pain and hurt. And then a load more had been chucked in, just in case, just in case there was any doubt in his head at all about where he was heading. Something reared up inside of him then, the angry black thing that had been growing and growing. He found the knife in his pocket, pressed his thumb on the blade until he felt wetness there.

When he took it out Moey didn't see it but the lad with the bruises did. JB watched as the smile fell from his face and then he stepped backward like the little lad. It was this motion that drew Moey's attention. His eyes fixed upon the knife but he didn't move. Instead he grinned again, a grin even wider than the one before.

'What you gonna do with that? Stab me with it?'

'Moey, let's go.'

The lad with the bruises was nervous.

Moey turned to look at him and then turned back. Once again his eyes settled on the knife.

'No way,' he said. 'He's a conman. He's had you all going but he's not having me.'

JB lifted the knife in front of him and Moey watched it, his eyes following its every move. JB watched it too. The light of the fire reflected off the blade. Behind Moey's head, the gang started to break apart.

After that it was a blur.

Moey went for the knife but missed. JB pulled back from him. The little lad jumped from the sea wall on to the beach to stay out of range, while the lad with the bruises teetered on the edge, undecided. Moey lunged a second time.

JB closed his eyes. The knife might have done nothing, just cut the evening air in two, or it might have done everything and caught Moey across the belly. He heard someone yelp and then he was turning away, scrambling up the beach, throwing the knife down, hearing it skitter across the pebbles.

He grabbed the petrol can and ran to the huts, splashed the petrol on to the porch of the first hut, threw the can at the door. It landed with a crash and settled. He got a stick from the fire and threw it at the hut, felt the rush of heat as the petrol took up the flame, and beyond the flames he saw Moey's gang scurrying up the beach away from the scene, feet slipping and sliding, hoodies closed over their heads.

And then JB was away from there too, running through the sea grass, running through the site, nipping behind his uncle's caravan as the policemen came out, skipping the fence, scrambling through the marshes, not caring where each step fell. He felt for his mobile in his pocket and lifted it out. The signal was bright and clear in the darkness. He still had the credit he'd saved for Sal but he dialled Carla now, loving the way his thumb fell on each number without him having to think about it, wondering how he'd ever started to feel that none of that mattered any more. He heard the ring-tone on the other end of the line, listened to the beauty of that sound, waited for the beauty of her voice.

36

'I'm coming back. I don't care what they say. It's our estate and . . .'

'Jay, it's not our estate . . .'

'We'll take it back then. We'll make it ours, like before. Things can be like they were before . . .'

'Things can't be like before. Things can never be like before. It's not ours any more. It can't be.'

'Yes it can. Just because they stick us under some curfew doesn't mean we all have to do what they say. If we stand up for ourselves there's nothing they can do. Why should they tell us when we can walk down our own streets? It's not fair.'

'Nobody cares about the curfew, Jay. We've not bothered with it. And nobody gives a toss about your ASBO either. All Scooby did was keep trying to get one.'

'Well then. We can get things back to before. What's up with you? Scooby won't be like this. When I speak to him he'll be well up for it.'

'Jay . . .'

'Think about it. Scooby, you, me, Dicko . . . the whole crew. It'll be sound.'

He was at the railway line. He'd already clambered through the wire fencing and scrambled up the slope to the edge of the track. Now he was by the rails, moonlight shining off the metal, the tracks leading away to the city. He was going back. He'd walk if he had to. Nobody was going to stop him, not the police, not Carla, not anybody. Way off in the distance, the single white light of a train heading his way. Let them try to stop him and he'd walk straight into the path of it.

The night was alive with sound, the sea rolling in and washing out on the beach, the distant wail of sirens, his uncle calling his name, the faintest singing on the line from the train, and Carla's voice,

'Something happened to Scooby, Jay. An accident. A bad accident.'

He didn't hear her. He listened to the singing on the line instead, listened to it grow, the light looming larger now, the sound of the sea rushing in his ears, washing over him, everything washing over him.

'Jay, I thought you knew. I thought they told you. I thought your mum was in contact. I couldn't do it. I couldn't make that call to you. None of us could. I thought you were calling to talk about it. Then you started talking about coming home and . . .'

The light ahead of him was brighter now, the singing in the metal, the music of angels calling out to him, calling for him to come to them.

'He took another car out, Jay. He smashed it up. We were all in it at first. We were talking about you, saying how we wished you were with us. Dicko said it was great how you'd taken the rap for last time. Then Scooby just flipped. He started ranting on about you and the whole thing with the ASBO. He wouldn't shut up about it. He said that you'd come up smelling of roses while he was still stuck. It wasn't nice, Jay. The things he said. He did too much green stuff this summer, every single night. It was messing with his head. He bundled us all out and raced off up the parkway. The blueys came around the corner and went after him. There was a helicopter, noise everywhere. We started back for the estate and about fifteen minutes later this ambulance raced by us. I knew straight away. I felt this chill go right through me. I watched the ambulance and knew it'd be too late. Jay, I'm really sorry. Jay? Jay? Jay?'

'Yeah.'

His voice was barely a whisper, the light blinding, the singing screaming.

'Jay, it's over. It's finished with.'

'It's not finished,' he said. 'It can't be finished.'

He was crying now, crying into the phone, clutching at it. The screaming turned to thunder. The light swallowed him. The mobile flipped from his hands and smashed to pieces under the wheels of the train, component separating from component, the train spewing each separate piece along the line, in the undergrowth, in the gravel, some pieces flying over the fence and on to the grass slopes, becoming lost there.

37

He spent the night by the tracks watching the flashing blue lights, listening to the men shouting across and back at each other in the darkness, staring at the water, at the fire burning orange in the night. Four of the huts were in flames already, sending embers drifting up into the sky, out over the water, reflecting off the water, a magnificent spectacle, sending out a message that told the world he was real and could do something people had to sit up and take notice of.

But he felt sick to the stomach each time Scooby came into his head. He couldn't shake the thought that kept rising up inside of him, Scooby was too good a driver, he would not crash a car, it didn't add up unless . . .

. . . he fought the idea, forced it back down, would not allow it access.

In the morning all that remained were the fragile skeletons of the first four huts, no longer distinguishable by their bright colours, just a dripping black heap of charred bones. JB watched the sea instead, watched the sunlight flicker and shimmer on the water until he felt ready to face it all, then he pulled himself to his feet and made his way back down the slope, back through the wire fencing to the site.

They were waiting for him when he got there, two groups of them, one at the site entrance, police cars parked up on the gravel, his uncle looking lost, a man in a suit that had to be Bellows; another man with them. It looked like Swallow. He couldn't be sure but he hoped it was Swallow. The second group was huddled together on the sea wall, grey mist rising in a cloud above their heads. Moey was there and the fat lad, the rest of them too, hooded and hunched, restless, switching and shifting from one foot to the other, switching and shifting back.

He pretended not to see anything, made his way towards the caravan. The dog came out to greet him and somebody shouted but he didn't stop. He was already locked in on something. It was on the steps, just sitting there waiting for him, a pristine white envelope, his name on the front. He picked it up and studied it nervously, trying not to get ahead of himself, trying not to imagine anything that could become a disappointment, but it *was* from her, it was her writing, it smelled of her.

Another shout. He looked up to see two of the policemen starting across the site towards him. He stepped back into the darkness of the caravan, the dog sniffing at his trainers, its tail wagging. Inside he opened the letter quickly, eager to have the moment before the next thing started up and carried him away with it.

One side of notepaper, a few short words, he didn't have a chance to take them in. It didn't matter. What mattered was finding it, knowing it was from her. He closed his eyes and listened to the sea-gulls crying on the wind, the breeze working its way through the caravan, somewhere beyond the sea lapping at the shore, delivering its rhythm, something that would be there tomorrow and the next day and the next day after that, something constant; something to test truths against.

There was running away from things and there was facing up to things. His father had done one thing, Carla too, even Scooby had done it in his own stupid way, and he was going to do the other. He would not run. He'd stay and take whatever they threw at him.

38

JB and his uncle spent the second week of September deciding what they wanted to keep from the caravan and take to the new place on the Watts Estate behind the beach road. In the third week a crane came and took the caravan away. It left a stain on the ground and a set of stone steps leading to nothing.

He was watching TV in the new place when Sal called. Ellie was sat with him, his mum and uncle in the kitchen, talking about the future.

'You got my letter then?' she asked.

'Yeah,' he said.

'What happened with everything?'

'My luck's changing,' he said. 'I didn't get the blame for any of it. My uncle told them there was a fire going on the beach and the wind got hold of it.'

'Good,' she said. 'Are you ready?'

'Yes,' he said.

He took the phone out back, slipped down the alley to the beach, hopped off the sea wall on to the pebbles, made his way to the surf line.

'Do you hear that?' he asked her.

'Yeah,' she said. 'It's perfect.'

'What now?'

'Nothing,' she said. 'Can you just stand there for a bit?'

'Okay,' he said.

'Thanks, Jay,' she said. 'It's true, what I put in the letter about that day.'

'I know,' he said. 'I believe you.'

'And you'll still be there in December? If I come back in the Christmas holiday you'll be there?'

'Yes,' he said.

'Promise?'

'I promise.'

'How's university?'

'It's all right,' she said.

'My mum wants me to go to college.'

'Are you going to do it?'

'I think so,' he said. 'Next year.'

'That's good,' she said. 'Let me hear it again.'

'Okay.'

He held the phone out in front of him, pointed it towards the water. He'd stand like that for as long as she needed him to. It was like she was with him, just the two of them down by the water, the waves caressing the shore, the sky wide open, the stars guiding them towards a better set of circumstances.

Merete Morken Andersen OCEANS OF TIME
£8.99   ISBN 1 904559 11 5

A divorced couple confront a family tragedy in the white night of a Norwegian summer. International book of the year (*TLS*), longlisted for The Independent Foreign Fiction Prize 2005 and nominated for the IMPAC Award 2006.

Michael Arditti GOOD CLEAN FUN
£8.99. ISBN 1 904559 08 5

A dazzling collection of stories provides a witty yet compassionate and uncompromising look at love and loss, desire and defiance, in the 21st century.

Michael Arditti A SEA CHANGE
£8.99   ISBN 1 904559 21 2

A mesmerising journey through history, a tale of dreams, betrayal, courage and romance told through the memories of a fifteen-year-old. Based on the true story of the Jewish refugees on the SS *St Louis*, who were forced to criss-cross the ocean in search of asylum in 1939.

Michael Arditti UNITY
£8.99   ISBN 1 904559 12 3

A film on the relationship between Unity Mitford and Hitler gets under way during the 1970s Red Army Faction terror campaign in Germany in this complex, groundbreaking novel. Shortlisted for the Wingate Prize 2006.

Booktrust London Short Story Competition
UNDERWORDS: THE HIDDEN CITY
£9.99   ISBN 1 904559 14 X

Prize-winning new writing on the theme of Hidden London, along with stories from Diran Adebayo, Nicola Barker, Romesh Gunesekera, Sarah Hall, Hanif Kureishi, Andrea Levy, Patrick Neate and Alex Wheatle.

Hélène du Coudray ANOTHER COUNTRY
£7.99   ISBN 1 904559 04 2

A prize-winning novel, first published in 1928, about a passionate affair between a British ship's officer and a Russian emigrée governess which promises to end in disaster.

Also available from
WWW.MAIAPRESS.COM

Sara Maitland ON BECOMING A FAIRY GODMOTHER
£7.99   ISBN 1 904559 00 X

Fifteen new 'fairy stories' by an acclaimed master of the genre breathe new life into old legends and bring the magic of myth back into modern women's lives.

Dreda Say Mitchell RUNNING HOT
£8.99   ISBN 1 904559 09 3

A pacy comic thriller about Schoolboy and his attempts to go straight in a world of crime. An exciting debut, winner of the CWA John Creasey Award 2005.

Anne Redmon IN DENIAL
£7.99   ISBN 1 904559 01 8

A chilling novel about the relationship between a prison visitor and a serial offender, which explores challenging themes with subtlety and intelligence.

Diane Schoemperlen FORMS OF DEVOTION
£9.99   ISBN 1 904559 19 0   Illustrated

Eleven stories with a brilliant interplay between words and images, exploring devotion in its many forms – to material objects, daily rituals, sensual pleasures, romantic love, even the status quo. A creative delight, rich in wit and irony, with playful, sometimes surreal, and often mysterious and unexpected juxtapositions. Winner of the Canadian Governor General's Literary Award.

Henrietta Seredy LEAVING IMPRINTS
£7.99   ISBN 1 904559 02 6

Beautifully written and startlingly original, this unusual and memorable novel explores a destructive, passionate relationship between two damaged people.

Emma Tennant THE FRENCH DANCER'S BASTARD
£8.99   ISBN 1 904559 23 9

Adèle Varens is only eight when she is sent to live with the forbidding Mr Rochester. Lonely and homesick, she finds a new secret world in the attic – but her curiosity will imperil everyone, shatter their happiness and send her fleeing, frightened and alone, back to Paris. An intriguing modern take on Brontë's masterpiece, *Jane Eyre*.

Also available from
WWW.MAIAPRESS.COM

Emma Tennant THE HARP LESSON
£8.99   ISBN 1 904559 16 6

With the French Revolution looming, little Pamela Sims is taken from her humble home in England to the French court, where she is brought up in a life of luxury as the illegitimate daughter of the beautiful Madame de Genlis and the Duc d'Orléans. But who is she really? Capturing the atmosphere of eighteenth-century France, her story reveals the complexity of a world where your origins create your identity. 'Riveting and very readable' (Antonia Fraser)

Emma Tennant PEMBERLEY REVISITED
£8.99   ISBN 1 904559 17 4

Elizabeth wins Darcy, and Jane wins Bingley – but do they 'live happily ever after'? Emma Tennant's two bestselling sequels to *Pride and Prejudice* are reissued for the first time in one volume. Ingeniously picking up several threads from Jane Austen's timeless novel, they take a lighthearted and affectionate look at the possible subsequent lives of the main characters.

Norman Thomas THE THOUSAND-PETALLED DAISY
£7.99   ISBN 1 904559 05 0

Love, jealousy and violence in this coming-of-age tale set in India, written with a distinctive, off-beat humour and a delicate but intensely felt spirituality.

Karel Van Loon THE INVISIBLE ONES
£8.99   ISBN 1 904559 18 2

Lawyer Min Thein has struggled to avoid confrontation with Burma's military regime, despite defending its victims. But when he incurs the wrath of the district commander, he is shadowed, intimidated and thwarted – he loses his country, his wife and his sight. A gripping novel about the life of a refugee, in which harrowing accounts of political prisoners blend with Buddhist myth and memories of a carefree childhood. 'This remarkable Dutch novelist is not just one to watch – he is one to live by' (*The Times*)

Adam Zameenzad PEPSI AND MARIA
£8.99   ISBN 1 904559 06 9

A highly original novel about two street children in South America whose zest for life carries them through the brutal realities of their daily existence.